FREDDY TO THE RESCUE

"Help! The Hamster Killer! It's outside my burrow! Help!"

The cry galvanised me, just as it had the first time. I froze once more, fur bristling. Everything inside me signalled a red alert.

First published in the UK in 2007 by Scholastic Children's Books
An imprint of Scholastic Ltd.
Euston House, 24 Eversholt Street
London, NW1 1DB, UK
Registered office: Westfield Road, Southam, Warwickshire, CV47 0RA
SCHOLASTIC and associated logos are trademarks and or registered trademarks of Scholastic Inc.

First published in Germany in 2000 by Beltz Verlag, Weinheim and Basel
Text copyright © Beltz Verlag, Weinheim und Basel, 2000
Illustrations copyright © Joe Cepeda, 2005
Translation copyright " Scholastic Inc, 2005
This edition published in the UK by Scholastic Ltd, 2007
The rights of Dietlof Reiche to be identified as the author of this work and Joe Cepeda to be
identified as the illustrator of this work have been asserted by them.

APPLE, MACINTOSH, and MAC are registered trademarks
of Apple Computer, Inc. Used without permission.

10 digit ISBN 0 439 95125 9
13 digit ISBN 978 0439 95125 8

British Library Cataloguing-in-Publication Data.
A CIP catalogue record for this book is available from the British Library

Printed and bound in Great Britain by Bookmarque Ltd, Croydon
Papers used by Scholastic Children's Books are made from wood grown in sustainable forests.

1 3 5 7 9 10 8 6 4 2

This is a work of fiction. Names, characters, places, incidents and dialogues are products
of the author's imagination or are used fictitiously. Any resemblance to actual people,
living or dead events or locales is entirely coincidental.

www.scholastic.co.uk/zone

CHAPTER ONE

THE CRY RANG OUT at twelve noon.

Well, I wouldn't swear it was twelve noon to the nearest second. We hamsters have a pretty accurate sense of time, but I happened to be asleep. We're "nocturnally active rodents", as the biology teachers call us, so we aren't exactly full of pep in the middle of the day.

I was curled up in my nest, dreaming. What I was dreaming of is beside the point (OK, it was the most delicious, succulent mealworm that had ever wriggled through *any* dream of mine – as big and fat as a cockroach grub).

So there I was, peacefully dreaming in my cosy nest.

And then that cry pierced my slumbers like a knife:

"*Help! The Hamster Killer – it's outside my burrow!* **HELP!**"

I sprang to my feet, fur bristling.

I was up in a microsecond because we hamsters

possess one of the most efficient alarm systems in the animal world.

I'm not boasting. I'm simply pointing out that my ears had registered every word of the cry while I was still asleep.

My ears?

It wasn't my *ears* that had picked it up! The cry had been uttered in Interanimal, the telepathic language in which all mammals (except humans) communicate.

But . . . in that case, I couldn't have been the only one to hear it. The other animals in the apartment must have done so too. Sir William and Enrico and Caruso must have been just as alarmed as I was.

Quickly, I crawled out of my nest, darted to the door of my cage, which is always open (Mr John would never dream of shutting it), and climbed down my little rope ladder to the floor (my home is on Mr John's bookshelf).

Then I scampered into the room next door.

Sir William is the biggest and blackest tomcat imaginable. He was lying on his blanket, fast asleep. Hadn't he heard the cry, or had he heard it and promptly dozed off again?

"Sir William?"

He didn't stir.

"Sir William!"

No reaction.

"Sir Will —"

"My dear Freddy, no need to yell like that." Sir William yawned, baring his huge fangs. They're a rather unpleasant sight from the viewpoint of a very small rodent like yours truly. However, Sir William can be trusted not to use them on me.

"I'm afraid I had to wake you," I said. "The thing is, I—"

"You didn't wake me." Sir William fixed me with his exceptionally green eyes. "Just because my eyes are closed, it doesn't necessarily mean I'm asleep."

True. It can also mean that he's philosophizing – meditating on the ways of the world. Or so he says. Except that I don't believe a word of it. Sir William is a civilized tomcat of impeccable character and wide experience, I grant you. But philosophizing means gaining new insights by logical deduction, and Sir William is about as good at that as Albert Einstein was at baseball. (Incidental note: of the four animals in this apartment, only one has a razor-sharp intellect.)

I took care not to say so to Sir William, of course. He believes he's practically perfect, and anyone who questions that belief out loud had better be an animal of Sir William's calibre at least. Purely physically, I mean.

"Sir William," I said, "I heard a cry just now. A desperate cry for help in Interanimal. I thought you must have heard it too."

He looked at me. "Freddy, if that were the case, do

you think I'd have remained lying here on my blanket, quietly meditating?"

No, Your Lordship, I said to myself. Not unless you were sound asleep and meditating in your dreams.

Sir William smiled indulgently. "You must have been dreaming, old boy." He closed his eyes, then opened them again. "Someone was calling for help, you say? What were this someone's actual words?"

I told him – and could have bitten off my tongue. It was obvious what Sir William would say next.

"'The Hamster Killer'?" He nodded complacently. "A typical golden hamster's nightmare, probably brought on by an overly heavy meal before bedtime. If I may make a suggestion: in the future, limit your supper to a morsel or two of lettuce. No cereals, let alone mealworms." He yawned. "And now, my dear fellow, permit me to resume my cogitations." He closed his eyes – and instantly fell asleep.

OK, so Sir William had slept through that cry for help. Or . . . might it have been a dream after all? My mental command centre had roused me, and it's usually as alert as a teacher on the lookout for someone passing notes in class. That meant the cry had probably been real, but there was an easy way of dispelling all doubt: I had only to consult Enrico and Caruso. Unlike hamsters and cats, guinea pigs are wide awake at noon. Those two were bound to have picked up the cry.

Except that there was a considerable drawback to this course of action: we weren't on the best of terms. Why not? Because, to put it mildly, Enrico and Caruso are guinea pigs of the most vulgar and impertinent kind. I'll say no more.

The fact is, they show me absolutely no respect – *me*, Freddy, not just any old rodent but the only golden hamster in the world who can read and write. In spite of this, Enrico and Caruso have the nerve to play tricks on me again and again! OK, enough said.

Well, not quite. Just to clue you in: I cannot only read and write, I'm also an experienced author. I've already, with my own paws, written two books on Mr

John's computer. And to think those comedians play their tasteless practical jokes on *me*, of all animals! OK, OK, Freddy, cool it. The long and the short of it is, I speak with them only when I have to.

All the same, someone had called for help. A HAMSTER WAS IN DANGER! A killer was after him! I had to go into action, but first I had to find out where the cry had come from. And that I intended to do, no matter how things stood between me and Enrico and Caruso, and however much I resented the fact that a hamster's survival might depend on them. I hurried off to their cage.

They were sitting side by side on their straw just inside the door, which was open. Caruso has short black-and-white fur. He's pretty big, even for a guinea pig, and fat on top of it. Enrico, who's smaller, has a long red-and-white coat concealing a rather scrawny body. Their expressions conveyed that they'd been expecting me.

"Hi," I said curtly, determined not to give them any

opportunity for one of their cheap wisecracks. "I'm sure you can guess why I'm here."

They looked at each other. Then Caruso shook his head. "Afraid not."

"We don't have the faintest idea," Enrico added.

So they were acting dumb. That probably meant they were planning some new guinea-piggery. But not with me — not with unflappable Freddy.

"OK," I said, "so answer me this: have you, or have you not, been awake for the last half-hour?"

They nodded.

"And you didn't hear something unusual?"

"Something unusual?" Enrico shook his head. "No, not a thing."

"Sorry, Freddy." Caruso spread his forepaws regretfully. "We were rehearsing a new number earlier on. Maybe that's why we didn't hear anything."

This was possible. Not even the most desperate cry for help would have stood a chance of making itself heard over one of their awful ditties — not even a cry in Interanimal.

"What *would* we have heard?" asked Enrico. "I mean, if we'd heard it?"

"It was a. . ." Stop, I told myself, don't be a fool! A cry heard by no one but me? What better excuse for sarcasm could I have presented them with? The least they'd have made out of it would have been a satirical poem — something along these lines: *So sensitive are Freddy's ears, he even ghostly voices hears. . .* No thanks, you guys. Count me out.

They looked at me expectantly. Now all I had to think of was some non-committal remark that would end my sentence on a cool, hamsterish note.

I was still deliberating when:

"*Help! The Hamster Killer! It's outside my burrow! Help!*"

The cry galvanized me, just as it had the first time. I froze once more, fur bristling. Everything inside me signalled **a RED ALERT.**

And Enrico and Caruso?

I stared at them.

They were still calmly hunkered down on their straw.

They sat there looking expectant, as before — as if no frightful cry for help had intervened between then and now.

"B-but," I stammered, "d-didn't you hear anything?"

They went on looking at me in silence.

And then, just as a vague suspicion was beginning to dawn on me, they exploded with mirth. They hooted with derisive laughter, flung their paws around each other, and rocked to and fro.

"That was the tops, Caruso!" squealed Enrico. "The absolute tops!"

"So much for supercool Freddy!" Caruso chortled. "Did you see the way I made him jump?"

"And his fur!" yelled Enrico. "It stood on end like he'd had an electric shock!"

I remained completely calm. Outwardly, I mean. Not a single whisker of my moustache quivered as I took in what they'd done. It was just about the lousiest practical joke since practical jokes were invented (no idea when that was; probably when the Almighty created guinea pigs). It had taken some doing, mimicking that cry for help just so I'd . . . mimicking it? Of course not! Caruso must have uttered the first cry as well!

OK, you guys, I said to myself, IT'S PAYBACK TIME. There was only one appropriate punishment: a double knockdown.

Enrico and Caruso had stopped laughing by now. They were sitting up on their straw, eyeing me curiously. As for me, I'd assumed a friendly, innocent expression.

All at once I reared up, inflated my cheek pouches, and bared my teeth in a menacing snarl.

Enrico and Caruso were so startled, they fell over backwards just like that.

It works every time. The two of them ought to have known what to expect, but they always forget, probably because a guinea pig's brain isn't programmed to cope with the sight of a hamster in fighting mode. Their alarm system hasn't a clue how to react, so they get a terrible shock and fall over backwards – and a good thing too. What isn't so good is that Sir William thinks it's unfair of me to flatten Enrico and Caruso like that. And when Sir William thinks something's unfair, a little rodent like me had better not do it.

Enrico and Caruso had just begun to scramble to their feet, grunting and groaning, when I heard: "Freddy, would you be kind enough to come with me?" Sir William came sauntering up. His Lordship had obviously gathered that I'd flattened the two of them, and now I was in for a severe tongue-lashing.

But this time, I said to myself, Enrico and Caruso had gone too far. When I told Sir William what a lousy, guinea-piggish practical joke they'd played on me, he'd be bound to——

"Help! Help! The Hamster Killer . . . aaahhhrrrggg. . ."

CHAPTER TWO

I COULDN'T HELP IT. My alarm system jolted me yet again, and this time the cry had sounded so frightful that every single hair of my coat stood on end. I must have looked like a terrified scrub brush. Caruso had really done a job on me this time.

Sir William was standing beside me with his eyes popping out of his head. His fur, too, was standing on end as if he'd stuck his paw into an outlet carrying five thousand volts. At least His Lordship's wrath would now be directed at the right person.

I looked at Enrico and Caruso.

HUH? WHAT WAS THIS?!

Enrico and Caruso were lying face down on their straw, flat as flounders. Their teeth were chattering so hard, it sounded like hail rattling against a windowpane.

"Th-that was g-ghastly," said Enrico.

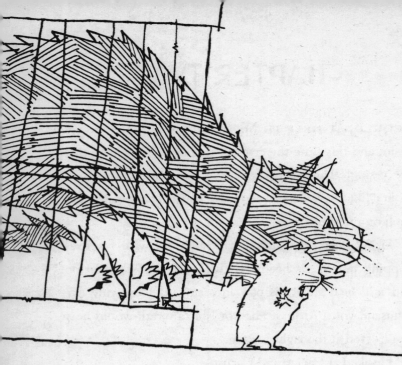

"It s-sounded like s-someone being m-murdered," said Caruso.

There was no doubt about it, they were quaking with sheer terror. The third cry had definitely not been theirs. What about the first? I had to find out right away.

"Now listen, you buffoons," I said sharply. I couldn't see the slightest reason for handling them with velvet paws. "You're going to tell me, in double-quick time, whether the first cry came from you — and stop that noise at once!"

They brought their jaws under control and eyed me resentfully. "After a cry like that," said Caruso, "anyone's teeth are entitled to chatter."

"I'm waiting for an answer!"

"The first cry wasn't ours," Enrico said.

"Nor was the third." Caruso glanced at Sir William, whose fur had flattened itself by now. "Only the second was mine."

"First cry, second cry, third cry — what's all this about?" Sir William looked at each of us in turn. "Would someone kindly explain?"

I enlightened him. What was more, I felt that I had every right to make a pointed allusion to Caruso's ventriloquism.

Sir William eyed Enrico and Caruso sternly. "That

was a thoroughly mean trick of yours. You should be ashamed of yourselves!"

They bowed their heads and gave an impression of two remorseful guinea pigs.

"All right," Sir William went on, "I'll leave it at that, in view of the urgency. We must now discover where the genuine cry for help came from." He looked at me. "Any ideas, Freddy?"

"No, none."

But something *had* occurred to me. What on earth was it?

I thought some more. How had the first cry gone? "*Help! The Hamster Killer! It's outside my burrow!*" Of course, that was a clue! "One thing I do know," I said. "Whoever was calling for help, it wasn't a *golden* hamster."

"Oh? What makes you say that?"

"Around here, golden hamsters live in cages. They can't dig tunnels, and they nest in hay or shredded paper.

16

Besides, a golden hamster would refer to his cage, not his 'burrow'."

"Very perceptive of you, my friend." Sir William looked down at me from his great height. "So in your opinion, what sort of hamster might it have been?"

I replied without thinking. No, it would be truer to say that the answer positively thrust itself on me. It emerged from my lips like a bullet from a gun:

"A FIELD HAMSTER!"

Within minutes I was on my way into Mr John's study.

Sir William and I had quickly concluded that this was a matter that far exceeded our animal capabilities. Besides, I'd discovered during recent events that consulting Mr John as soon as possible was not only wise but could make the difference between life and death. Enrico and Caruso kept their mouths shut while Sir William and I conferred. They had obviously grasped that the very last thing we needed at this moment was a comic turn. They may also have felt slightly ashamed of their latest practical joke (about as ashamed as a rainstorm is of wetting someone).

Mr John was seated in front of his computer, typing away. I climbed the little rope ladder leading from the floor to the desk and sat up on my haunches.

"Hello, kid." Mr John gave me a nod. He has a big nose and big, bushy eyebrows. He went on typing, so I pointed at the screen.

"Got something to tell me?"

I nodded.

"OK." Mr John saved what he'd written and blanked out the screen for me. "But make it snappy, kid. I'm behind with my work."

I nodded again. *This is an emergency,* I typed. Even though I have to press each key down with my forepaws, one at a time, and run from one

18

key to the next, my message came up on the screen quite fast. I could have used a shorter word than *emergency,* because it meant darting from the E to the M and back. Being an educated golden hamster, however, I prefer to converse with Mr John on his own intellectual level. (Of course, it would be simplest if humans communicated in Interanimal like every other species of mammal.)

"AN EMERGENCY?" said Mr John. "Here in the apartment?"

No, not in the apartment, I typed. *Somewhere outside.* I proceeded to describe the two cries for help. (Only the genuine ones. I didn't mention Caruso's, not wanting to burden Mr John with the knowledge of such a lowdown, guinea-piggish trick.) The cries had been in Interanimal, I went on, and explained why I was convinced that they'd come from a field hamster, not a golden hamster. Moreover, the second cry had probably been uttered on the point of death.

"Hmm," said Mr John. "Two questions, kid."

Mr John always has two questions, and he always

19

puts his finger on the doubtful aspects of a story. (There are two doubtful aspects to every story, if not more.)

"First, why a field hamster? There are other kinds. Couldn't it have been a pygmy hamster? A pygmy hamster living in a very large cage filled with earth? Earth he'd dug himself a burrow in?"

Hmm, there was something in that. Why hadn't it occurred to me? Probably because I can't take any rodent smaller than a golden hamster seriously. On the other hand, I was sure of my facts.

It was *a field hamster,* I typed. *A golden hamster's senses are infallible.*

"Well, er, if you say so." Mr John eyed me. "Second question: were there only two cries?"

I nodded.

"And they probably came from some field or other," he continued, "from far away?"

I nodded again.

Then he said, "I'm wondering why you aren't absolutely swamped with cries for help."

How so? I typed.

"Look, kid, there must be thousands of animals in trouble in this city alone – animals in fear of pain or death. Thousands of them must be putting out distress calls in Interanimal at any one time." Mr John looked at me. "So why don't you hear them *all?*"

Yes, why didn't I? Why wasn't my brain seething with cries for help?

I don't know, I typed, *but maybe we ought to think about that some other time. One thing we do know: somewhere or other a field hamster was being murdered, and where there's one there must be more.* **We've got to save them.**

"You're right, kid." Mr John nodded. "The question is, where are they?" He pondered for a moment. "Let's try the Internet. Maybe we'll find something under 'field hamster'."

The result was shattering. We not only found something, we found a list of precisely 360 websites in which the key words *field hamster* occurred. Mr John sighed. "By the time we've ploughed our way through that lot. . ." He sighed again, and I added under my breath: ". . . all those hamsters will be dead."

"Well, this'll get us nowhere." Mr John wiped the list off the screen. "We've got to do something *pronto.*" He looked at me. "Know something, kid? We ought to let Linda in on this. But only if it's OK with you, of course."

100%, I typed, and he reached for the phone.

Linda Carson is Mr John's girlfriend. I have to admit that, although I've learned a lot about humans in the course of time, I still find it hard, as a hamster, to assess the relationship between them. Between a male and a female, I mean. When two hamsters share a nest and have babies together, their relationship is obvious. But Linda Carson and Mr John live in separate nests – apartments, I mean – and they don't have any babies. The fact remains, Linda and Mr John are a couple.

Linda is a reporter, and this was her last day at the *Daily Chronicle*. She was due to start work with a local TV station the next day.

"Linda?" said Mr John. "Hi. Mind if I pick your brain about something? I can't explain how I learned it, not right now, but it involves some field hamsters that may be in danger. . . What's that? An agency report came in this morning? You don't say! . . . Yes, I'm speaking from home. . . Fine, see you then." He hung up.

"She'll be here in half an hour." Mr John hesitated, then he said, "Listen, kid, I'll have to explain how I knew about those field hamsters. That means. . ."

. . . *letting her in on my secret,* I typed.

He nodded. "But I think it'll be at least as safe with her as with me."

My secret was the fact that I, Freddy the golden hamster, can read and write. Mr John had thought it wise from the start to keep it under wraps, arguing that I might wind up in the hands of some scientist eager to dissect my brain. (I did, unfortunately, but that's another story.) Anyway, we'd agreed not to tell another living soul about my secret.

Not even Sophie.

Sophie was my mistress before she handed me over to Mr John (because her mum is allergic to my fur). When Sophie was doing her homework, she'd let me have the run of her desk, and because she was learning to read, I learned too. Even I was amazed at how easy I found it, and I soon developed a hearty appetite for reading matter. But how to get at some books? I wasn't allowed to roam around the apartment, and Sophie always shut me up in my cage after finishing her homework.

Why didn't I simply tell her? Because she didn't possess a computer, and a hamster's paws are too small to cope with other writing implements like pens or pencils. I did, for all that, snitch a pencil from her.

Why? Because I needed something to prise open the door of my cage. That solved my reading-matter problem – or rather, it would have solved it if Sophie's mum hadn't developed that allergy to my fur the next day. But then I was relocated to Mr John's apartment, and here, where reading matter was concerned, I'd ended up in an Aladdin's cave.

I've kept the pencil. It's still where it used to be, buried in the litter on the floor of my cage. Sometimes, when I'm in the mood for a trip down memory lane (we golden hamsters can get pretty sentimental when we feel like it), I dig the pencil out. It's made of unvarnished, unpainted wood, and it feels nice between the teeth — pleasantly soft but firm. I have a chew at it, sighing a little as I ponder the old days, then I bury it once more.

Sophie comes to see me quite often, incidentally, and it's heaven whenever Mr John's study becomes pervaded with her fragrant personal aroma of sunflower seeds. Besides, she regularly presents me with a mealworm. Sometimes even two.

Mealworms feel even better between the teeth than pencils. Best of all, though, you can bite them in half. When you do, your mouth fills up with a taste so sublimely delicious that, to be frank, I can't understand why humans don't sample such delicacies themselves.

But Sophie's visits always leave me feeling a little sad as well. How dearly I'd like to show her my poems! I write poems, you see. They're golden-hamsterish verse of the most sensitive kind, and I'm planning to publish them. I already have a title: *A Hamster in Love*. I can't use my own name, of course, so I'll have to think of a pseudonym. No one must know that the author is a genuine golden hamster. That's why Sophie too, can't be allowed to . . . HEY, JUST a MINUTE!

I'd almost forgotten: Mr John and I were on the point of disclosing my secret! He'd proposed that we share it with Linda. What objection was there to sharing it with Sophie as well? None! On the contrary, if anyone deserved to be informed of my exceptional talents it was Sophie. After all, it was through her that I'd learned to read.

AT LAST!

At last, I would be able to show her my poems and reveal my true feelings for her. It would herald an entirely new phase in our relationship. **FREDDY MEETS SOPHIE! FANTASTIC!** I leaped into the air and turned two somersaults in quick succession (another of my talents).

"Hey, kid!" Mr John laughed. "What's got into you all of a sudden?"

Joy, I typed. *Unbridled joy at the thought that I can communicate with Sophie at last.*

"Hmm." Mr John stroked his chin. "You mean you think we should let Sophie in on this too?"

I nodded.

He gave me a long look. Then he slowly shook his head. "Sorry, kid."

???, I typed.

"It won't do." He shook his head some more. "We can't afford to share your secret with Sophie."

27

CHAPTER THREE

I STARED AT MR JOHN, mute and motionless.

I must have looked as if an icy gust of wind had abruptly frozen me into immobility like a hibernating animal. I felt that way too.

But then rage — hot, hamsterish rage — came welling up inside me.

How dare Mr John tell me what I could and couldn't do?

It was time to remind him of something in the strongest terms: Sophie had come into my life before Mr John, so what gave *him* the right to forbid me to communicate with her?

I bared my teeth and prepared to snarl.

"Listen, kid," he said. "I can't forbid you, I don't have the right, but I'd like to

convince you that letting Sophie in on your secret would be dangerous."

If I put myself at risk, I wrote, pounding the keys with my paws, *that's my business!*

Mr John nodded. "Sure, kid, but not if you endanger other people as well."

Like who? I typed, still fuming.

"Like Sophie herself."

Five minutes later, my rage had evaporated. Not entirely, though. A little resentment lingered – more than a little, in fact.

Still, Mr John had made it clear to me that I really would be endangering Sophie if I let her in on my secret. "She'd never give it away on purpose, of course," he said, "but she's very young. She'd let it slip sooner or later. And then," he went on, "it wouldn't be long before some evil-minded character appeared on the scene. It wouldn't be the first time."

OK, Mr John, you've got a point, I typed. *We'll only tell Linda, then.*

But there was enough room between "You've got a point" and "I quite agree with you" for a fair amount of resentment. My rancour was directed not only at Mr John but, strangely enough, at Linda too. I had to let off a bit of steam somehow.

So today, for once, I decided not to give Linda one of my special welcomes.

But when she walked into the study, a slim young woman nearly as tall as Mr John, with lustrous red hair and a personal aroma of apple and peach blossom so fragrant that any hamster could be excused for swooning with delight, my resolution melted like a Popsicle in the sun: I sat up and begged, raised my right forepaw, and waved (a trick perfected by no other golden hamster in the world).

"Hello, Freddy," Linda said in her soft, melodious voice, which sounded so pleasant to a hamster's ears.

"Did you sleep well? Did you dream of something nice? A mealworm, perhaps?"

I never ceased to be amazed by her ability to read a hamster's mind. To demonstrate my affection for her, I turned a somersault.

Mr John chuckled. "He likes you, that's quite obvious."

"And I like him." Linda looked at me. "A shame we can't communicate in some way. I wish we could."

THaT MaKeS TWO OF US, LaDY. And you've no idea how soon your wish will come true.

Linda was still looking at me intently, almost searchingly. I wondered why.

Suddenly, she turned to Mr John. "And now, John, I want an explanation. How did you know those field hamsters were in danger?"

"Well, er, um. . ." Mr John indicated the chair in front of his desk. "Better sit down."

"Why? I'm OK the way I am."

"But you may not be for much longer. I mean, not when you've heard what I'm going to tell you."

"Oh?" Linda slowly subsided on to the chair.

"Well. . ." Mr John had clasped his hands behind his back. "I know it takes a lot to shake you, but I didn't want to spring this on you out of the blue."

"Very considerate of you." Linda was now regarding him as intently as she'd stared at me before. "I'm really not a shrinking violet, though, so spit it out."

But Mr John, who was determined to break the news gently, refused to be hurried. "Well, er," he said, "to borrow from Shakespeare, 'There are more things in heaven and earth,' Linda, 'than are dreamt of in your philosophy.'"

"Hmm." Abruptly, Linda sat up very straight. "And what, my dear John, would I never have dreamed of?"

"OK, fasten your seat belt." Mr John seemed to have shifted up a gear. "Look at Freddy, please."

Linda looked at me. I couldn't interpret her expression, but she was obviously in a state of extreme suspense. At the same time, however, I thought I detected a faint smile on her lips.

"Sitting there the way he is now," Mr John went on, "Freddy looks like a perfectly normal golden hamster. On the other hand, he can do something a normal golden hamster can't – and I don't mean wave or turn somersaults." He paused. "This is very difficult," he muttered.

"John," Linda said quietly, "are you trying to tell me that Freddy can read and write?"

It took Mr John precisely a minute to recover his composure.

He was thrown right off balance. To begin with, he stared at Linda as if she'd told him she wasn't an Earth dweller but an extraterrestrial. Then he started muttering, "I can't believe it!" over and over.

When he'd muttered it for the third or fourth time, Linda said, "Come, come, John, I've never seen you so flabbergasted."

"Sure, I'm flabbergasted," he said. "What shocks me is how easy you found it to crack Freddy's secret."

"Easy?" Linda shook her head. "It was anything but. I couldn't help noticing a few things, but it was far from easy to draw the right conclusion from them."

"Things? What things?"

"That little rope ladder leading to the desktop, for instance. There isn't any hamster's gym equipment up there, let alone any grain or mealworms." I was enveloped in an intoxicating cloud of apple and peach blossom perfume as Linda bent over me. "So what would a golden hamster want with a computer?"

What indeed, lady? The cloud of perfume was making my head swim.

Linda smiled. "Shall we try to have a conversation, Freddy? Any objections?"

I seemed to float through the fragrant cloud to the

keyboard. *Absolutely none,* I typed. *First, nice to speak with you. Second, never change your perfume!*

Linda laughed. "I promise," she said.

"But, Linda," said Mr John, shaking his head, "if you knew Freddy's secret – or guessed it, at least – why did you never say anything?"

She shrugged. "The two of you had obviously decided not to confide in anyone, so I kept my mouth shut."

I must insert something here. We male golden hamsters are notorious loners who prefer to live on our own. If we do share our nest with a female, she has to be a really good sport – one who keeps her nose out of matters that don't concern her. From that standpoint, Mr John is to be congratulated on his choice of a girlfriend.

"These field hamsters," said Linda, "– how did you hear about them? Does it have anything to do with Freddy's secret?"

"It certainly does," said Mr John. "And now we'll let you in on another secret. That is, unless you know it already."

Needless to say, Linda had never heard of Interanimal. She was pretty surprised, but not so surprised that it knocked her sideways.

Mr John proceeded to tell her about the two cries for help and my theory that they'd been uttered by a field hamster.

"Freddy may well be right," Linda said. She took a sheet of paper from her shoulder bag. "This is the agency report I received this morning. I'll read it to you." Which she did.

Don't worry, I'll tell you what it said in a minute, but first I must state something for the record – most emphatically, if I may: we golden hamsters (Latin name: *Mesocricetus auratus*) are the crème de la crème of hamsters, so to speak. You can forget about pygmy hamsters, likewise field hamsters (Latin name: *Cricetus cricetus*), even though they're at least three times our size. Why? Because field hamsters are uncouth peasants. All that interests them is filling their bellies. How do I know this? I was told it by Great-Grandmother, and

36

Great-Grandmother wasn't just anyone. It was she who initiated us youngsters into the secrets of hamsterdom in the cage where I was born.

So we were dealing with a colony of field hamsters. I confess that, once I'd grasped this, I briefly toyed with the thought of leaving them to their fate. Why should I, a golden hamster, care what happened to a bunch of hayseeds? But OK, I decided otherwise. After all, field hamsters might be country dwellers, but they were, in a manner of speaking, cousins of mine. I only hoped they deserved my help.

And now, here is the agency report Linda read aloud:

"FIELD HAMSTERS — A FALSE ALARM.

"Fears that a new automobile plant could not be built because the site earmarked for it was inhabited by field hamsters have proved to be groundless.

The mayor's office at first thought it possible that the development area was occupied by a colony of field hamsters. Had this been true it would have meant curtains for the new automobile factory. Field hamsters, being threatened with extinction, are a strictly protected species, so approval of the factory's construction would have had to be withheld.

"However, the mayor announced yesterday that a scientific inquiry had discovered absolutely no trace of a hamster population on the site. All objections to the factory have thus been eliminated.

"Meanwhile, a group of animal rights campaigners has cast doubt on the scientists' findings in an e-mail addressed to our news agency. These anonymous militants, who call themselves 'The Muskrats', have announced that they intend to prevent construction work from taking place. Excavation of the factory's foundations, which is scheduled to start today, will therefore be carried out under guard."

There was a brief silence when Linda finished reading.

Then Mr John said, "Sounds fishy to me."

"It stinks to high heaven," Linda agreed. "Those cries for help are proof of the hamsters' existence. The scientists are lying."

"But why should they?" asked Mr John.

Linda looked at him. "Are you being serious?"

"Well, er. . ."

"I know you believe in the essential goodness of humanity, John, but to me the whole thing's as plain as the nose on your face: the mayor has decided in favour of the factory and against the field hamsters. THEY'LL BE EXTERMINATED."

"Hold on." Mr John thought for a moment. "That Freddy heard cries for help is one thing; that there may be some field hamsters living on the construction site is another. That the two things are connected is only a theory."

"A theory with a lot going for it," said Linda. "You're right, though. What we need is confirmation, and I know how to get it."

"Really? How?"

"I'll ask the mayor himself – I'll interview him. And, just so he can't pull the wool over my eyes, I'll invite a hamster expert of my acquaintance to come with me."

Till then I'd only been listening, but now I couldn't resist asking a question. *You mean, you know a hamster expert?* I wrote across the screen.

"Sure. He's the best too."

How interesting, I typed, feeling annoyed. I phrased my next question in suitably sarcastic language: *And who, pray tell, is he? May one be permitted to know the name of this immensely distinguished expert of yours?*

"Sure," said Linda. "His name is

FREDDY."

CHAPTER FOUR

I'D MEANT TO COME OUT with some smart ideas on the subject of experts, but I was feeling rather ashamed of myself, so I refrained.

"Well," said Linda, "will you come to see the mayor with me? As my expert, I mean?"

Be glad to, lady, I typed. *He may not play ball, though.*

"That's a strong possibility." She grinned. "However, we'll think of something. And now —"

She broke off. The phone was ringing.

"Hello?" said Mr John. "Oh, it's you, Sophie. . . Of course, you can pay us a visit. When? Fine, see you then." He hung up. "Sophie's coming over. Is that OK with you, Freddy?"

A visit from Sophie OK with me? What a question! Instead of replying on the screen I turned a somersault.

"That was plain enough!" Linda laughed. "I must get

back to work. I'll try to make an appointment with the mayor right away."

"Let's hope no more hamsters are murdered in the meantime." Mr John escorted her to the door.

Sophie was coming!

I scrambled quickly down the rope ladder to the floor, dashed over to the bookshelves, and climbed the rope ladder to my cage. Feeling sentimental for some reason, I unearthed the pencil from my litter.

Ah yes, the pencil – the thing that had gained me my freedom, the lever I'd used to prise open the door of my cage. When, I wondered, had I begun to long for freedom?

Was it when Great-Grandmother
taught us that a hamster's fodder
really should, as well as food,
mental sustenance include?
Was it then that little me
felt a yearning to be free?

Was it when the fates decreed
I should quickly learn to read?
Was it when I learned to write
on an iMac in the night?
Was it then that little me
gained a love of liberty?

No! Such questions are in vain.
Only one thing can explain
what transformed my hamster's lot:
the smell of sunflower seeds, that's what,
for their scent can only mean
little Sophie's on the scene.

I've called this poem "Meditation on a Pencil". It will come at the beginning of the volume of poetry I'm planning (that's right, the one titled *A Hamster in Love*). In my opinion it's golden-hamsterish verse of the highest quality. I can't wait to hear what the critics make of it.

And Sophie?

She won't be able to give an opinion on it because I can't show it to her – because she'll never discover what Freddy the hamster really feels for her.

If golden hamsters could weep, I would by now (I confess) have shed a tear or two. As it was, I merely chewed the pencil and brooded. It felt good but did little to raise my spirits. Still in a melancholy mood, I buried the pencil once more.

But Sophie's arrival banished my dejection, and all was as it should have been. To begin with, at least.

She came dashing into the study accompanied by an alluring scent of sunflower seeds. **"HELLO, FREDDY!"** she called.

I sat up in the doorway of my cage, made myself as tall as I could, and waved to her.

"He's waving!" Sophie exclaimed. "He's saying hello!" She's always so delighted, anyone would think it was the first time I'd done such a thing. She was already producing a paper bag from her pocket.

I've discovered that Sophie goes to immense trouble over my mealworms. She fattens them on lettuce leaves, rolled oats, and heaven knows what else, which means that they grow to a size of which the ones on sale in pet shops can only dream. The mealworm Sophie deposited on my feeding place that day was one of the biggest and fattest under the sun. I bit into it at once. (I'll spare you the details because I'm aware that many humans are repelled by a mealworm's squirming exterior, let alone its succulent innards.) Then, when I'd polished it off, I performed my customary somersault of delight. And that was precisely when sorrow engulfed me once more. I would never be able to express my feelings for Sophie except by waving and turning somersaults! For once, one

of Enrico and Caruso's satirical songs had hit the target
fair and square:

> "His lovesick heart throbs in his breast,
> his little knees go weak.
> He waves his tiny paw at her.
> Ah, would that he could speak!
> She smiles at him and says hello,
> but he can only squeak."

Dejectedly, I hunkered down on my litter, thankful
that Sophie couldn't tell what I was feeling at that
moment.

"And now, Freddy," she said, "I've got a surprise for
you. I've brought you something else today."

I straightened up.

She felt in her pocket. "I wanted to give you a special
treat, but I didn't know what. Then I remembered how
you used to scamper around on my desk. There was
something there you'd set your heart on. You kept

pestering me, so in the end I let you have it." She withdrew her hand from her pocket. "This isn't the same one, of course, but it's similar."

It certainly was. The same thickness, the same length, and – most important of all – the same unvarnished, unpainted wood. It was just like my lever pencil!

Linda's car was one of those economical little compacts that are only good for short trips from A to B, but

47

which, when they get to B, always manage to find a parking space. Mr John had squeezed into the passenger seat with his knees drawn up. I was sitting on the shelf at the rear, so that I could see out. Not that I could see much. Golden hamsters aren't blessed with superlatively good eyesight, I'm afraid, but mine was good enough to watch Linda and Mr John. And watch them I had to, if I wanted to get the full flavour of their conversation. You see, humans don't communicate only by speaking to each other. Without being aware of it, they do so by waving their hands around and making faces as well.

Also on the back shelf was Linda's laptop (so that I could, if need be, write something on the way), and on the seat below were her shoulder bag and a big camera case.

"I don't know." Mr John shook his head. "The mayor will never believe I'm a press photographer. I'm hopeless at taking pictures."

"You don't have to take any pictures, John. Just pretend, OK?"

"I wonder why he's invited us to his home instead of City Hall."

"He says it's more convenient for him." Linda shrugged. "What's the difference? I'm going to interview him, that's the main thing. He was very reluctant at first, by the way. He didn't agree to be interviewed until I said it was about the field hamsters – then he caved in pretty quick. I think my best plan will be to tackle the subject head-on."

"Probably," said Mr John. He pondered awhile. Then he said, "How do you take a portrait photo? From the front, or in profile? It depends on the shape of the person's face, I guess."

"John!" Linda said impatiently. "You're only impersonating a photographer so we can smuggle Freddy in, OK? Anyway, I want to coax the truth out of him, that's all. His personal appearance doesn't matter a row of beans."

Mr John shook his head. "You're wrong. The way people look is a good indication of the way they think and act."

"You could be right," said Linda. "If I remember correctly, the mayor is a short, fat, bald-headed cigar smoker."

The mayor was a short, fat, bald-headed pipe smoker.

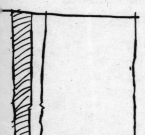

I peered cautiously out from under the lid of the camera case. Mr John had put it down on a side table. He was standing not far away, busily pretending to take pictures.

The pipe smoke might prove a problem. My nose was already tickling.

Linda was seated in front of the massive desk, on which she'd deposited her tape recorder. Behind the desk, ensconced in a huge leather

50

swivel chair, sat the portly mayor. His friendly, open smile was that of a man with absolutely nothing to hide.

Or everything.

"Well, Miss Carson, what was it you wished to know?"

"Your Honour," Linda began politely, "a certain construction site was believed, not without good reason, to be occupied by a colony of field hamsters. And then — PRESTO! — the creatures suddenly vanished. How come?"

The mayor continued to smile. "Because there never were any hamsters. Scientific inquiries have proved it."

"Definitely?"

"Definitely and beyond all doubt. The report is signed by a team of recognized experts." The mayor's smile widened. "I'll be glad to let you have a copy."

"Thanks, that won't be necessary. I'm sure the report is airtight." Linda seemed to be thinking things over. "So everything's OK, and there aren't any problems," she said. Then swiftly added, "In that case, why did you agree to this interview?"

Mr John, who was at the point of pretending to take a picture, lowered the camera.

"Well, er, because. . ." The mayor picked up a box of matches and proceeded to relight his pipe. This took some time. Then he said, "The answer's quite simple. As you know, some militant animal rights campaigners continue to claim that there are hamsters living on the construction site. I want the public to be quite clear. I expect this interview to yield a newspaper article that will dispose of the hamster question once and for all."

"I'm sorry, Mr Mayor," said Linda, "but it's no use."

"Er . . . I'm afraid I don't quite understand."

"I won't be writing any such article. On the contrary." Linda paused. "We have an expert's report of our own."

The mayor sat up straight. **"AN EXPERT'S REPORT?"**

"Yes, and it proves beyond doubt that there *are* some field hamsters living on the site."

"Really? May I ask who produced this report?"

"You may, but don't expect an answer. We naturally

won't divulge the name of our expert – he enjoys the confidentiality due any informant – but I'll tell you this much: he's an expert whose knowledge of the subject is second to none. In any case. . ." She broke off.

Someone had knocked on the door.

"Yes?" called the mayor.

A woman entered. Tall and bony, with her grey hair knotted into a bun, she was carrying a tray of coffee things.

The mayor frowned. "I told you to wait till I rang, Martha."

"I know you did." Martha strode over to a low table with some chairs grouped around it. "But in case you'd forgotten, it's my afternoon off." She plunked down the tray with a crash.

"Thank you, that'll do. You can go."

"Have a nice day," said Martha, and she strode out as resolutely as she had marched in.

"My housekeeper." The mayor smiled. "A dragon with a heart of gold. Well, a cup of coffee can't hurt. Feel free." He remained seated behind the desk, lighting his pipe yet again, while Linda and John helped themselves to some coffee.

I'd never seen anyone smoke a pipe before. The confounded thing kept going out and smelled worse each time it was lit. It was all I could do not to sneeze.

"Very well," the mayor said abruptly, "you leave me no choice. Miss Carson, would you ask your photographer to step outside?"

Linda hesitated, then nodded to Mr John. He put down his coffee cup and went out, leaving me and the camera case behind.

"Well. . ." The mayor had got his pipe going again and was puffing out clouds of smoke. "What I'm now going to tell you is not for publication. Would you mind turning off that tape recorder?" he asked amiably. "In a way that will convince me you've done so?" he added.

Linda raised a little flap and shook four batteries on to the desktop.

The mayor nodded. "You're a professional, I see. All

54

the better. It means I can level with you." He smiled broadly. "You asked why I agreed to this interview. The fact is, I wanted to find out how much you knew. Well, I now know you possess an expert's report of your own. You know about the hamsters."

A long pause.

"Miss Carson," he went on, "you realize you can't use anything I tell you from now on?"

Linda nodded. "Of course. If I did, you'd swear you never said it." She hesitated. "All that puzzles me is why you're going to tell me anything at all."

"I'll be glad to explain." The mayor sat back in his chair. "I don't want you making trouble for me and my friends. Get this straight: you'd be wasting your time coming to the hamsters' rescue and writing articles condemning the automobile factory. The inevitable will happen. You can't prevent it."

"AND WHAT WILL HAPPEN?"

The mayor laid his pipe aside and folded his hands. "Miss Carson, hundreds of jobs are dependent on this new factory. I ask you: what do a few dozen hamsters matter compared to that?"

At that moment the tickle in my nose became irresistible: **i SNEEZED EXPLOSIVELY.**

Silence fell. I held my breath.

Then the mayor said, "We'll soon get rid of a few dozen hamsters."

He hadn't heard me sneeze after all.

CHAPTER FIVE

WE LAUNCHED "OPERATION COUSINS in Distress" the same afternoon.

By "we" I mean yours truly seated on the back shelf of the car as before, Linda in the driver's seat, Mr John with a map spread out on his knees in the passenger seat, and finally, beside me on the back shelf, Sir William and — sad to say — Enrico and Caruso.

Sir William lay stretched out with his head on his forepaws and his eyes shut. From time to time he uttered a faint, plaintive mew.

"Oh, dear," he'd muttered soon after we drove off, "I don't think cars agree with me. I feel sick." After a while he groaned, "I hope I won't disgrace myself." Since then he'd just lain there in silence, bravely fighting off his nausea.

Enrico and Caruso, on the other hand, were in fine fettle. Seated side by side on the back shelf, they watched the scenery flashing past (for some unaccountable reason, guinea pigs have been endowed by nature with pretty sharp eyesight) and belted out a succession of songs from their repertoire. The noise was appalling. In the end I couldn't stand it any longer.

"Honestly, you guys, can't you show a bit of consideration for Sir William?"

"Enrico," said Caruso, "I do believe His Hamstership dislikes our singing."

"In that case, buddy, there's only one thing for it. One, two, three. . ."

And they chanted in unison:

"When Freddy puts his paw down
it means he's laid the law down,
and we are very much afraid
that Freddy's laws must be obeyed."

Somewhere, probably in the furthest reaches of outer space, there must exist some sinister being that advises those two comedians on the best way to bug me.

I trembled with rage – suppressed rage. The last thing I wanted was to show them how thoroughly they'd infuriated me. "Listen," I said, "your humour is in very poor taste. We're engaged on a serious mission. Hamsters' lives are at stake."

"But of course!" Enrico slapped his forehead. "How could we have forgotten! *That's* why we're on our way!"

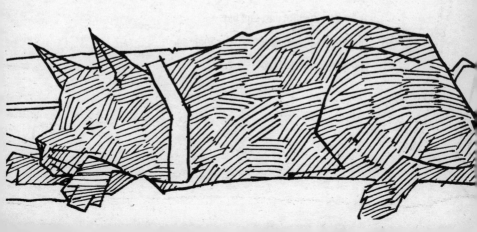

"Yes indeed!" Caruso spread his paws in a theatrical gesture. "We're on our way into the blue! This calls for a song, Enrico — a song appropriate for the occasion. One, two, three. . ."

And off they went again — at the top of their voices:

"Life's an adventure, friends, and we
would ne'er its risks and dangers flee.
Let those who wish to, stay at home,
but we prefer the world to roam.
'Will you come too? By all means do so,'
say Enrico and Caruso.

But would a hamster heed that call?
We doubt it. Hamsters are too small
and timid, but a guinea pig
is brave, adventurous, and big.
'Freddy, stay home, you're wise to do so,'
say Enrico and Caruso."

Hamsters small and timid? The sinister being from outer space had struck yet again! I stood there, teeth bared and fur bristling. How dare their lousy song mock me for my size and question my courage? Had I ever made personal remarks about guinea pigs? Had I ever mentioned their slipshod attitude to personal hygiene, for instance, or the fact that Enrico and Caruso's cage is, to call a spade a spade for once, a total pigsty? OK, YOU GUYS, GET READY. The sinister being from outer space is in for a lesson.

They were sitting with their backs to the rear window, which meant they would crack their heads on the glass when I flattened them. Maybe it would knock a little sense into their skulls. I drew myself up.

"My dear Freddy," said Sir William, "be fair. That song of theirs was genuinely amusing. I'm feeling a good deal better now." He turned to Enrico and Caruso. "Thank you, boys."

Sir William is what you'd call a personality, there's no denying it, but he's got as much sense of humour as a mealworm being devoured by a hamster. That's how he came to appoint Enrico and Caruso as his personal entertainers. Ever since then, those two jokers can spout any old garbage that comes into their heads – His Lordship is bound to be amused.

In fact, I suspected that the only reason Enrico and Caruso were in the car at all was that Sir William didn't like to go anywhere without his court jesters.

62

*　*　*

When our grand council of war had decided to launch Operation Cousins in Distress (the name was my idea), no immediate consideration was given to the question of who should take part in it, only to what we could actually achieve — if anything.

"We can forget about newspaper articles," Linda said. "By the time I get one published, the hamsters will have ceased to exist. The mayor has kindly decided to exterminate them."

I nodded. (We animals were all sitting on Mr John's desk, incidentally. Sir William had jumped up there, and because guinea pigs are as good at climbing as sacks of potatoes, Mr John had lifted Enrico and Caruso on to the desktop.)

"Hmm," said Mr John. "What if we go to court? What if we take out — what's it called? — an injunction or something?"

"We'd have to prove that the mayor's scientific report is phony," said Linda. "For that we'd need to call our own expert witness, and I'm afraid the judge wouldn't let Freddy testify."

"In that case," said Mr John, "we've got only one option. We'll have to round up the field hamsters from the construction site and take them somewhere else."

That would be difficult, Mr John, I wrote on the monitor. *Finding them would be hard enough.* As things now stood (the excavation work had already started), the field hamsters wouldn't be running around outside; they'd have taken refuge in their burrows. We would have to work out an evacuation plan – with their cooperation, of course. *And that's when things would get really difficult,* I pointed out. *From what I've heard, my cousins are cussed, quarrelsome animals of the first order.*

"Hmm," Mr John said thoughtfully. "Well, I suggest we go there first and see how things turn out."

Linda nodded in agreement.

"Who else will be going?" asked Enrico.

He'd said it in Interanimal, of course, so Linda and Mr John couldn't hear, but it was a question we animals would have to settle among ourselves. I decided to nip any arguments in the bud.

"Aside from me," I began, "I think that—"

Caruso cut me short. "He wasn't asking you," he said. "He was asking all of us."

"Freddy, my friend," Sir William chimed in, "Caruso's right. This is a decision to be made jointly."

"OK," I said, "then here's what I suggest: the only ones to go on the operation are those who are really needed."

"Agreed," said Enrico and Caruso.

Great. That meant the two dopes had ruled themselves out.

"Freddy will be going, certainly," Sir William ordained. **"He's our expert."**

"The only trouble is," said Enrico, feigning deep concern, **"he's on the small side."**

"Which means," said Caruso, looking equally worried, "that the size of the construction site will present him with a serious transportation problem."

And the two of them broke into a mocking chorus:

> "Our hamster expert likes to brag
> but suffers from an awkward snag:
> he cannot travel far, alack,
> unless he rides on pussyback."

They'd sprung one on me yet again, but this time I kept my cool. Carry on, you guys, I said to myself. You don't know it yet, but *you're* the ones who'll be staying behind.

From the practical aspect, unfortunately, Enrico and Caruso's gibes were justified. Being small, the only way I can cover long distances is to cling to the back of Sir William's neck with my teeth and let him carry me. And here I'd like to make another statement for the record: it's extremely decent of Sir William to volunteer to do this every time.

I looked at him enquiringly.

"But of course, old boy," he said with a nod. "I'll be happy to give you a lift as usual."

So it only remained for me to tell those two comedians where they got off. "Sorry, you guys," I said sympathetically. "Much as I regret it, you'll have to stay behind. Unless," I added, "you can produce some argument in favour of your taking part in the operation?"

"Sure we can," said Enrico.

"What do you mean?"

"I mean we can be useful," said Caruso.

"Oh yeah? How?" I was really curious to hear. They could hardly cite an ability to crack tasteless jokes.

"We can dig," said Caruso.

"You can what?!"

"Dig," Caruso repeated. "Your cousins live in underground caves, right?"

I nodded.

"Then the operation may involve digging."

"You say you can *dig*?!" This was the height of

impertinence. Hamsters can dig, and so, maybe, can a few other kinds of rodents, but *guinea pigs?* "With your pathetic paws," I said as scornfully as I could, "the most you can do is root around in pee-sodden straw."

"Freddy," Sir William broke in sternly, "the two of them say they can dig. Unless or until they're proved wrong, let's give them the benefit of the doubt. Agreed?"

"Hmm," I said.

"And now, my dear Freddy, I'd be much obliged if you would inform Mr John that we'll all be going together."

CHAPTER SIX

IT WAS STILL LIGHT when we reached our destination around six thirty. The construction site, which lay on the edge of a wood not far from a village, was simply vast.

"Gee," sighed Mr John, "finding the hamsters here will be like looking for a needle in a haystack."

"I had no idea an automobile plant covered so much ground," Linda said dejectedly.

We were hiding on the edge of the wood to escape detection by security guards. Linda had parked the car some distance from the site for the same reason, and Mr John, to spare Sir William, had carried me there in his pocket with Enrico and Caruso perched on his shoulders. There was no sign of a nighwatchman.

"Look over there, where those earth-moving machines are parked," said Linda. "Nothing's going on there either."

"Still," said Mr John, "they've already started bulldozing this field."

I couldn't see that far. But Linda had already turned on her laptop, so Mr John put me down in front of the keyboard, and I was able to type a question: *What sort of field is it?*

"A grainfield. Only just harvested, from the look of it."

This must be the place, I typed. *Let's start looking.*

I was seated on Sir William's back with my teeth buried in his furry neck. The guinea pigs, who followed on foot, proved surprisingly nimble, even plump Caruso.

We'd decided to start by crossing the field diagonally in hopes that we might discover something right away. It had been agreed in advance that we animals would conduct the search by ourselves while Linda and Mr John lay low. We arranged to rendezvous on the edge of the wood in an hour's time and discuss what to do next.

Mr John had estimated that the grainfield (it was a wheat field, incidentally) was roughly the size of two football fields. A pretty vast area by my standards, but at least, it sounded manageable. I felt confident that, if any of my cousins lived there, we would find them.

"What exactly are we looking for, Freddy?" asked Sir William.

"Holes in the ground," I said, "holes big enough to take Caruso with ease." That was what Sir William and the guinea pigs were to keep an eye out for. I, on the other hand, was searching with my nose. I had no idea what my cousins smelled like, but of one thing I felt certain: if I picked up their scent, I would know it right away.

"Hey, over there!" Sir William said suddenly. "A HOLE!"

He was right! I slid off his back to the ground.

It was a hamster's burrow – the exit tunnel, to be exact. You could tell that from the way it sloped upwards. The entrance, which would have led straight down into the ground, had to be somewhere nearby.

73

I drew in some air through my nose: the smell pattern was unchanged. No new scent had appeared.

Enrico and Caruso were peering down the hole. "Hey!" Enrico called. "Anyone home?"

"Forget it," I said, "that burrow is unoccupied." Sir William lowered his head, and I climbed on again.

"I strongly advise you not to yell like that in the future," I warned the guinea pigs. "If a field hamster felt provoked, it could end in tears. For you two, I mean. Field hamsters use their teeth without mercy, so keep your traps shut."

Enrico and Caruso snapped to attention. "YESSIR!" they barked in unison.

"Listen, you guys," I said, controlling myself with an effort, "I'm being serious. Don't pick a fight with those characters, and for heaven's sake don't try one of your

comic turns. My cousins have no sense of humour, I assure you. Unlike me," I added.

"Yessir!"

"OK, OK, have it your own way. You'll soon see what I—"

"Freddy," Sir William broke in gently, "I think we ought to continue our search."

The next hole we found was another exit tunnel. I checked the smell pattern again, and this time it had changed. A new scent had announced itself, but so faintly that its source was unidentifiable. The mental alarm bell I expected to hear when I came across my cousins failed to ring.

"What now?" asked Sir William.

"Maybe I should go down there and take a look," I said thoughtfully.

"But be careful, old boy. What you've told us about your cousins doesn't exactly fill me with confidence. Are you positive they wouldn't attack you too?"

"To be frank, Sir William, no."

"Wouldn't it be better if I came with you?"

"Aside from the fact that the tunnel is too small for you, I hardly think it would help me to establish contact with my cousins if I turned up with a tomcat in tow."

"True." Sir William grinned.

"Hey," Enrico called from a few feet away, "we've found another hole!"

"That'll be the entrance!" I called back. "Don't go too close!"

"It leads straight down into the ground!" I heard Caruso exclaim.

"Exactly!" I called. "That's why I'm telling you not to—"

"WHOOPS! HELP! Aaaieee..."

"Caruso?" That was Enrico. "Hey, where have you gone? Caruso? Whoops! Help! *Aaaieee...*"

Silence.

After a few seconds, Sir William said, "That seems to settle it, old boy. You'll have to take a look yourself."

I nodded. "**SHAKE PAWS**, Sir William, and let's pray that the burrow is unoccupied."

I slithered down the entrance tunnel – and found myself in the realm of the field hamsters!

Realm, of course, is an exaggeration. It was merely the burrow of a solitary hamster and also – I hoped for Enrico's and Caruso's sake – an unoccupied one. The fact remained that I'd entered an alien world. Cautiously, I made my way along the downward-sloping tunnel. It was exceptionally wide and roomy. I myself could never have dug a burrow of such dimensions. I felt like someone in a fairy tale who had suddenly been transported to the land of giants. Not only the burrow but everything else seemed huge – the tree roots, for instance, and that mealworm over there. I stopped short. No, it wasn't a mealworm, it was an enormous maggot! My, what a whopper! And the scent of it! Should I. . . ? No, first I had to find Enrico and Caruso. I walked on.

The scent of the maggot lingered a while. Then another scent joined it – the one I'd faintly detected outside. It grew stronger and stronger until it suddenly overwhelmed me. I came to a halt. That was it, my cousins' scent!

I can't pretend it was very fragrant.

Gingerly, I continued on my way. All at once I heard something, and that something made me fear the worst for Enrico and Caruso. It was an unmistakable snarl.

Coming to a bend in the tunnel, I peered around the corner. And there, where the tunnel widened out into an underground chamber, it stood.

IT WAS A GIANT.

I mean, my readers must try to imagine what it would be like to come face to face with a fellow human three times their size. That was how the field hamster looked to me, a golden hamster.

It had risen on its haunches, blown out its cheek pouches, and bared its teeth in a snarl. But . . . it wasn't a he, it was a she – a female cousin, not a male! Why hadn't it ever occurred to me that my cousins could be of both sexes? Never mind. I was confronted by a gigantic, snarling female hamster. She didn't just sound angry, she sounded *extremely* angry.

Lying in front of her on the floor of the cave were Enrico and Caruso. They were down on their backs with their paws in the air – begging for mercy, or so it seemed, and I felt sure it would take a minor miracle to save their skins. I feverishly racked my brains. What minor miracle could I perform?

Suddenly, in addition to the snarl, I heard another sound. The sound of sobs. Enrico and Caruso were sobbing. The sobs grew louder – no, they turned into chuckles: Enrico and Caruso were chuckling with suppressed amusement! The two of them were on the verge of roaring with laughter. **GREAT HEAVENS!** Nothing could save them now, not even a *major* miracle.

Enrico and Caruso continued to chuckle. "With respect, Your Frightfulness," they spluttered, "you can let the air out of your cheeks."

"We're only two comedians passing through."

"Passing through," chortled Enrico, almost beside himself, "but not passing water."

That did it. They both exploded into squeals of merriment.

I turned away, not wanting to see what would happen next.

But . . . what was that?

A deeper sound had mingled with their raucous laughter – an unmistakable, **"HO, HO, HO!"**

The giantess was laughing.

She bellowed with laughter, long and loud, clutching her stomach as she did so.

"Two comedians passing through!" she roared. "Not passing water. . ." And she rocked with mirth.

I breathed a sigh of relief. Not only for Enrico's and Caruso's sake, but because it now seemed that our mission would be easier than I'd feared. My cousins obviously had a sense of humour (guinea-piggish humour, at least), so they couldn't be as difficult and troublesome as all that. Feeling reassured, I came out from behind the bend in the tunnel.

I have to admit that, at that moment, my hamster's instinct for danger must have deserted me completely.

Either that, or I was so relaxed that my alarm system had simply switched itself off.

Whatever the truth, I approached the lady hamster without a second thought.

Her instincts were in excellent working order. An outsider in one's burrow?! When that happened, any hamster who didn't happen to be dead or dumb was bound to adopt the most menacing stance possible.

The giantess loomed over me, cheek pouches bulging like pumpkins, razor-sharp teeth bared in a hissing snarl.

Making a run for it was out. She would have pounced on me in a flash, and then farewell Freddy! So my alarm system jolted me into an equally menacing posture, except that it was pretty unimpressive compared to hers. If things got physical, it was obvious who would come off worse.

"No, Your Awesomeness, don't!" cried Enrico. "He's quite harmless!"

"It's only pathetic little Freddy," Caruso chimed in.

One thing was clear: if I survived, those guinea pigs had better make their wills.

The giantess let the air out of her cheek pouches. "Freddy?" She had stopped snarling. "That's a funny name. A really funny name." Suddenly, she gave another roar of laughter. "Funny little Freddy! What a scream!"

"Yes indeed, Your Hilarity," said Enrico. "He's the funniest little hamster in the world."

"By the ridiculous name of Freddy," Caruso added.

If I survived, they wouldn't even get a chance to make their wills.

The lady hamster's mirth subsided. She stopped laughing and settled herself comfortably on her haunches. She didn't look so enormous sitting down. "Hello there, Freddy," she boomed, but that, I presumed, was her normal tone of voice. "I'm Elvira. So you're the leader of this troupe of entertainers, are you, you funny little pygmy hamster?"

Pygmy hamster! My first contact with the field hamster colony hadn't taken a particularly flattering turn from my point of view. As for me being the leader of a troupe of entertainers, I had to put a stop to that idea as soon as possible, or I could kiss Operation Cousins in Distress goodbye.

"Ahem!" I cleared my throat commandingly. "Esteemed Cousin Elvira," I began, "we're here because—"

"Ah, me," warbled Enrico, "Elvira is my heart's desire!"

"And mine," warbled Caruso. "She sets my blood on fire!"

"Ho, ho, ho!" laughed Elvira. "What a couple of characters you are! Which one of you is which?"

Enrico and Caruso replied in turn, bowing low, and sang the last two lines together:

> "Enrico is the name I bear,
> and I am called Caruso.
> If we can serve Your Ladyship
> we'll definitely do so."

"Your Ladyship, yet! Ho, ho, ho!" Elvira's vanity was clearly tickled.

"Listen, Elvira," I began again, "we're here because——"

"Boys, I've taken a fancy to you," she boomed at the guinea pigs. "In fact, I like you a lot."

I'd been ignored – brushed aside. Great! Instead of launching my rescue operation, I was being compelled to watch a couple of stupid guinea pigs suck up to a female hamster with a voice like a bullhorn.

i HAD TO THiNK OF SOMETHiNG FAST.

And I did.

"Help! The Hamster Killer! It's outside my burrow! Help!"

CHAPTER SEVEN

ELVIRA SHOT TO HER FEET SO FAST, her head nearly hit the roof of the cave. Her fur, far longer than mine, bristled like a porcupine's, and she bared her razor-sharp teeth again — this time in terror.

Enrico and Caruso had assumed the frightened guinea-pig posture: they lay belly down with their teeth chattering.

Suddenly, however, the chattering ceased.

They stared at me.

"What's the matter, boys?" I asked.

"Caruso," said Enrico, "I don't get it. Was that Freddy yelling?"

"It was, Enrico, and you know something? I'm rather disappointed in him."

"I'm mega-disappointed, Caruso. Who would have thought him capable of such a cheap and unimaginative way of getting back at us?"

Elvira had hunkered down and was looking from one to the other. "What *is* all this? Can someone explain?"

"It means," I said quickly, before Enrico and Caruso could get a word in, "that the cry came from me."

Now it was Elvira's turn to stare at me. "But . . . but . . . it sounded like Rosco."

"Rosco? Would that be a hamster who was murdered earlier today?"

She nodded. "He was crushed to death in his burrow. But . . . how could *you* know that?" Suddenly, she straightened up. "Who are you? Where do you come from?"

Good question, Elvira. You might have asked it right away instead of flirting with a pair of dopey guinea pigs. "We're from the city," I said, "and we want to help you."

"From the city? To help us?" Elvira looked at Enrico and Caruso.

"This isn't a comic turn," I said firmly. "We've come to save you from the Hamster Killer."

"Huh?" Elvira shook her head. "Forget it. Nobody's a match for the Hamster Killer. All we can do is pray."

At that point I thought "All we can do is pray" was merely the kind of thing people say without really meaning it. I was soon to discover that it signified a whole heap of trouble. "Well," I said, "*we* think something can be done."

Elvira shook her head again, very determinedly this time. "The Hamster Killer is an enormous tractor unlike any we've ever seen before. It makes the ground shake, and the huge shovel on the front digs so deep, no burrow is safe from it." She added that two of her neighbours, Jasper and Lulu, had lost their burrows that very morning. They'd escaped by the skin of their teeth, unlike poor Rosco. "All we can do is pray that the Hamster Killer will go away."

"No," I said rather impatiently. "Praying won't help, I guarantee you. The construction site –" I broke off.

Something had suddenly dawned on me: these field hamsters knew nothing about the projected automobile plant – how could they? All they knew about was their burrows and the wheat field. They didn't have a clue what went on in the outside world. They collected grain and any other food that came their way, filled their store chambers during the summer, and hibernated in the winter. Their way of life, I now realized, resembled that of my golden hamster ancestors long ago. That they were acquainted with tractors, unlike my ancestors, was hardly surprising. After all, their wheat field was ploughed, sown and harvested by machines every year.

"Praying doesn't always help," I told Elvira. "Suppose the Hamster Killer doesn't go away? We ought to prepare for that eventuality." I hesitated. "All of us together, I mean."

"Hmm," said Elvira.

"Do you think there's any chance of holding a meeting? I realize," I added quickly, "that you field hamsters lead strictly solitary lives."

She nodded again.

"But perhaps, just for once, you could get together?"

"We do," she said.

"Do what?"

"Get together." Elvira thought for a moment. "In fact, we'll be meeting in half an hour."

"In half an. . ." My jaw dropped. "You mean, you'll all be getting together? Every last member of the colony?"

"Yes, all of us. We'd have met today in any case. Because today. . ." She paused. "Today is the Seventh Night."

Elvira was reluctant to disclose what she meant by the term "Seventh Night". "It's too long a story," she said. "You'll see for yourselves."

"Can we attend the meeting uninvited?"

"No, not uninvited," she said. "But Fronso can't object if *I* invite you."

"Fronso?"

"Our priest. Be patient, you'll see."

Their *priest*? I was growing thoroughly uneasy, I'm bound to admit.

Enrico and Caruso were untroubled by such emotions. They spent the remaining time buttering up "Fair Elvira", as they now addressed her. I'll spare my readers the details.

At last, she said, "Well, time to go." She had previously stuffed her cheek pouches with grain and peas from one of her larders. When I asked whether the meeting place was so far away that rations were needed for the journey (a little joke of mine), she merely uttered an impatient grunt. But why, I wondered, was she taking so much food along?

Elvira led the way back to the entrance tunnel and turned off down a side passage.

What followed was an exhausting trek. I'm not the weakest of animals (I work out regularly on the gym equipment in my cage), but some distances are just too great for the likes of me to cover on foot. It wasn't long before my paws became thoroughly sore. I didn't utter a word of complaint, though, if only to avoid any snide remarks from Enrico and Caruso, who were bringing up the rear. But our forced march seemed endless.

At long last, Elvira came to a halt. We were not far from the point where the tunnel ended. "Wait here," she said. "I'll have a word with Fronso first." And she disappeared.

Cautiously, I made my way towards the end of the tunnel to see where it led. Peeking around the corner, I

found myself looking

out into a regular underground cathedral,

a cavern higher and wider than I could ever have

imagined. It must have taken generations of field hamsters to excavate it.

Several dozen of my cousins had already assembled there. Seated at intervals on the floor of the cavern, they seemed at pains to keep at least two paws' lengths from their neighbours, but all had positioned themselves so that they could look at the same spot.

Their eyes were fixed on the centre of the cavern.

And there, on a circular pedestal moulded out of clay, stood a **JaR.**

It was a big-bellied earthenware jar with handles on either side and a lid on top. Its outer surface was discoloured – covered with dirty brown blotches, which indicated that it must have lain buried in the ground for many years before being dug up.

Also on the pedestal were numerous mounds of grain and peas. Like Elvira, the other hamsters had brought food from their larders and deposited it around the jar.

I spotted Elvira near the pedestal, talking earnestly to

a hamster a good deal smaller than herself. Though he had a sizable paunch, I noticed.

She left him and made her way back to me. "Fronso was reluctant at first," she said, "but I convinced him that he had to grant you a hearing. I'll introduce you when the time comes. Then you can tell us how to save ourselves from the Hamster Killer."

I nodded.

"As for you two," she went on, turning to Enrico and Caruso, who had followed me to the mouth of the tunnel, "you'd better keep out of sight. Too many outsiders at once might make Fronso and the others nervous."

The guinea pigs obediently withdrew.

"Why is Fronso your priest?" I asked Elvira. "I mean, why him in particular?"

"Because he was born in the burrow where the JaR OF HOPE was found a long time ago. All our priests have come from that burrow since time immemorial."

"And what's all that food lying around the, er, Jar of Hope?"

"It's a sacrificial offering designed to influence the Jar of Hope in our favour. Most of my fellow hamsters believe that the jar swallows it, or they'd never give up any of their precious stores." Elvira looked at me. "Of course, Fronso snitches it all himself when everyone's gone." She shrugged her shoulders. "I don't mind too much. I tell myself it's his fee for the banquet."

"The banquet?"

"The Banquet of Hope. Quiet now, it's starting."

No longer looking at the jar on the pedestal, the assembled hamsters transferred their attention to Fronso, who had mounted a second, smaller pedestal and was sitting up like a dog begging. He really was quite small for a field hamster, and his haunches were overhung with rolls of fat.

"Beloved hamsters of the field!" Fronso scanned the members of his congregation one by one. "Like your ancestors of old," he went on in an oily but penetrating voice, "you have come together on the Seventh Night to partake of the Banquet of Hope – to pray for a good harvest and well-filled larders. Today, however, we pray for something else as well: the disappearance of the Hamster Killer." He raised his paws. "Let us pray."

100

The hamsters gazed once more at the jar pedestal in the centre.

"O Jar of Hope!" Fronso intoned. "Unto thee we lift up our eyes. Hear us! In thee, noble Jar, repose our dearest hopes. Thy precious contents will not fail us."

"Thy precious contents will not fail us," the hamsters repeated in unison.

"Partake, therefore, of the Banquet of Hope!"

"We partake of the Banquet of Hope," chanted the congregation.

Then they sang:

"Jar of Hope, to thee we pray,
we will ne'er thy trust betray.
May we ever rue the day
if we fail our dues to pay."

I watched these proceedings with very mixed emotions, I admit. On the one hand, they made me feel thoroughly sentimental. I recalled how Great-Grandmother had told us youngsters about the Promised Land of Assyria, the paradise that all golden hamsters hope to attain someday.

On the other hand, it exasperated me that these field hamsters were swallowing every word fat Fronso uttered, and that they should worship that old jar so ardently, many of them in absolute ecstasy. Even Elvira was looking rapt. Heaven alone knew what they thought the jar contained. Some may have been thinking of all the good food they believed to be stashed away inside it; others may have envisioned its contents as a host of delicious maggots.

"Beloved hamsters of the field!" cried Fronso. "Rest assured: the Jar of Hope has heard your prayer. The Hamster Killer will disappear." He spread his forepaws. "Go forth, therefore, with joy in your hearts." He got down off the pedestal. The Banquet of Hope on the Seventh Night was at an end.

The members of the congregation had already turned to go when Elvira hurried across the cavern and mounted the priest's pedestal. "Hamsters of the field!" she boomed.

They all stopped short and looked at her.

"We have a visitor — a cousin from the city." Elvira beckoned me to join her on the pedestal, which I did. A murmur rose from the hamsters.

"THIS IS FREDDY!" Elvira cried. "Don't be misled by his size." Louder still: "Freddy knows how we can save ourselves from the Hamster Killer!"

Just then my eye fell on Fronso. He was standing beside the jar, with the sacrificial offerings all around him, glaring at me.

The hamsters sat down again and looked at me expectantly. I cleared my throat. "Hamsters of the field," I cried, "there's only one way to save yourselves from the Hamster Killer." I proceeded to explain what a factory was ("Tractors have to be manufactured somewhere"), then what an automobile was, and finally that the humans had decided to build an automobile factory here on their wheat field. "They're aware of your existence," I said, "but the factory will be built regardless. In other words, the Hamster Killer won't leave until you've all been crushed to death." I surveyed my audience. Most of them seemed to have understood; many even nodded. "There's only one answer!" I cried. "You must abandon this field and find yourselves a new one."

They all stared at me.

Then a loud voice broke the silence:

"He's Lying!"

CHAPTER EiGHT

FRONSO WAS STANDING amid the sacrificial offerings with his paws upraised. "This pygmy hamster is trying to fool you!" he cried.

Pygmy hamster! Slowly but surely, that inaccurate description was getting on my nerves.

"The Hamster Killer will disappear," Fronso declared. "That's certain, because the Jar of Hope has heard your prayer. So why does this pygmy hamster want us to abandon our field?"

Yes, why? I was genuinely interested to hear his answer.

So were the field hamsters. They had all turned to Fronso.

"Because the pygmy hamster and his tribe are after your food, that's why! They're too small and lazy to gather any for themselves. They plan to raid your larders at their leisure!"

Raid their larders?! I was thunderstruck.

All the field hamsters turned back to me, and I can't say they looked particularly friendly. I had to think of something that would win them over again, and fast.

"Hamsters of the field!" I shouted. "It's Fronso who is lying! He's the one who snitches your—"

"Are you going to let the pygmy hamsters rob you?" cried Fronso, and his voice, I regret to say, was a great deal more penetrating than mine. "Look at him, hamsters of the field! There he is! There stands the lying, greedy pygmy hamsters' errand boy!"

Many of the field hamsters – most of them, in fact – had bared their teeth. Then, with horrified disbelief, I saw them begin to move in my direction. Slowly, but with lethal intent, they advanced on me. Where was Elvira? On the pedestal beside me, but she too, had bared her teeth. It was clear that, like the others, she now regarded me as a greedy pygmy hamster. My route to the exit tunnel was temporarily blocked by furious,

murderous field hamsters. Elvira drew herself up and prepared to pounce. I shut my eyes.

AND THEN IT HAPPENED.

Just a faint tremor at first.

But the tremor became a shudder. The cavern shook — the vast chamber shook so hard that clods of earth fell from the roof. I lost my balance and tumbled off the pedestal. The field hamsters near the exit tunnel had fled. I dived into the tunnel and started running.

107

But the shaking didn't stop. The ground continued to shudder under my paws as I sprinted along. Then came a rumbling sound. Instantly, I drew in my head and curled up into a ball. Another rumble, then. . .

SILENCE.

After a while I raised my head.

The tunnel was pitch-dark and smelled of freshly turned soil. I cautiously groped my way forward. Almost at once, my whiskers detected a mound of earth extending to the very roof of the passage.

I turned around and groped my way back. After only a few steps, I came up against another mound of earth. The tunnel had caved in behind and ahead of me.

I WAS TRAPPED.

At first, this didn't alarm me too much. I was a golden hamster, after all, and equipped with paws ideally suited to digging.

I promptly set to work on the wall of earth ahead of me – and just as promptly stopped. A sharp pain had transfixed my paws. Of course, they were already sore from that long trek! I'd been unaware of the pain all this time, but it had now come with a vengeance. I had to extricate myself, though, and pretty quickly, because the air in the tunnel would soon run out.

I gritted my teeth and set to work once more. What had Great Grandmother taught us? "A hamster's paw must dig till it's raw." But that iron-willed-old-lady hamster's motto and reality were two different things. I stopped again, less because of the pain (although it was agonizing) than because I realized that if I went on digging like crazy, my paws would soon be quite useless. All the same, I had to get out somehow. . .

What was that?

A scratching, scraping sound! Faint at first, it grew steadily louder until it came from just beyond the wall of earth ahead of me. There was a sudden glimmer of light, an opening appeared, paws thrust the earth aside, and. . .

"YOO-HOO!"

called Enrico. "There he is, our little pygmy hamster!"

"No, Enrico," Caruso said reproachfully, "he's an author, not a pygmy hamster."

"You're right," said Enrico, feigning remorse. "How could I be so tactless?"

For a moment, I'd actually rejoiced at the sight of the pair, but my feeling of joy had lasted no longer than it took for Enrico to call "Yoo-hoo!"

"Listen, you guys," I said, limping over to them. "I know you're here to rescue me, but that doesn't—"

"Correct me if I'm wrong," Enrico broke in, "but weren't we all supposed to be of some use to this operation?"

"We were," said Caruso. "So where does that leave poor, paw-sore Freddy?"

And they broke into song:

"Our celebrated author's paw
is used to lighter work by far.
He'll burrow into nice, soft straw
and pound the keyboard hour by hour,
but when a tunnel's to be dug
he winds up feeling far less smug."

Then, heedless of the fact that I'd just escaped suffocation by a hair's breadth, they actually had the gall to burst into squeals of laughter.

Trembling with suppressed fury, I debated how to repay them for their tasteless behaviour.

"Freddy," said Enrico, "don't you think we should concentrate on what really matters?"

I stared at him.

"We really don't have time to indulge in personal animosities," said Caruso. "We must get to the surface as quickly as possible."

That took my breath away. They'd bushwhacked me with a logical argument for once! Someday, I would take a trip into outer space and have a word with their sinister adviser in his lair — even if his lair was in Galaxy 999.

It was still light when we reached the surface, although it had taken us quite some time to find an unoccupied burrow whose exit tunnel we could use. The cavern containing the Jar of Hope had not collapsed, as luck would have it. We encountered no field hamsters there. Fronso had disappeared, and so had the sacrificial offerings on the pedestal.

We did not, of course, emerge at the spot where I'd left Sir William. It would take a while to find him, and it was almost time to rendezvous with Linda and Mr John as we'd planned.

Upon regaining the surface, we were greeted by a sound I couldn't identify – a low rumble interspersed with squeaks and rattles. Caruso craned his neck. "There's a machine going backwards and forwards over there."

"YES," said a voice, "it's a BULLDOZER."

"Sir William!" I exclaimed. "How did you get here?"

"On foot, my dear fellow." He gave a self-satisfied smile. "I kept on combing the area because I had to assume that you wouldn't emerge at the spot where you disappeared."

He reported that the bulldozer had driven straight across the field — hence the earthquake in the cavern — but that he had managed to get out of its way in time. It seemed that work on the construction site was proceeding at night as well. The bulldozer was now operating some way off. "All the same, old boy," Sir William concluded, "we're rather pressed for time."

He went bounding off across the field with me perched on his back and clinging to his furry neck with my teeth. I felt certain I was steering him straight for the spot on the edge of the wood where Linda and Mr John would be waiting. (A golden hamster's sense of direction is legendary.)

Enrico and Caruso had returned to the field hamsters' subterranean realm, their cursory explanation being that the hamsters had no quarrel with *them*. In fact, it was obvious why they were braving the risk of another cave-in. Given a big enough audience, those conceited guinea pigs would have put on a show with the whole world collapsing around their ears.

The course I'd set for the spot on the edge of the wood proved accurate to the nearest inch.

"Are you quite sure, my dear Freddy?" queried Sir William. "I can't see any sign of Mr John or Miss Carson."

Neither could I, but my markers – a hazel bush and

a maple tree – coincided perfectly with the images I'd stored in my brain. The smell pattern matched as well. There was only one answer.

"They must have gone," I said.

"You think so?" Sir William shook his head sadly. "That would be disastrous." Suddenly, he looked up. "Someone's coming!" He pricked his ears. I could hear it too, the sound of footsteps made by human feet in boots. But also by paws — a DOG'S PAWS.

"Hang on tight with your teeth, Freddy!" Sir William hissed, and he raced up the maple tree. Once he reached a fork invisible from the ground, he crouched down. "There they are," he whispered.

The human was a young man in a kind of uniform. The basic colour was black, but his neckerchief and belt provided an agreeable touch of colour. The dog, which was on a leash, made a less agreeable impression. It was a huge, vicious-looking Rottweiler. We could thank our lucky stars we were well out of reach.

They had just walked past beneath us when the young

man
retraced
his steps and
sat down with his back
against our maple tree. "Dinner
break," he said, taking a packet of
sandwiches from his pocket.

How long was a dinner break? Time
was getting tight.

The dog had sat down
beside its master. "It's a
lady dog!" Sir William
whispered suddenly.

I was about to ask
what difference this
discovery made to
our predicament
when we were
hailed from below in Interanimal: "Hey, you up there. No
point in hiding, I smelled you long ago."

"Really?" said Sir William. "And what exactly did you smell?"

"You're a tomcat," replied the Rottweiler, "and your companion is a rodent of some small variety. A pygmy hamster, maybe."

"For Pete's sake!" I blurted out. "I'm a GOLDEN hamster."

"Whatever. But allow me to introduce myself: my pedigree name is Princess Sonia of Maryland."

"Charmed, Your Highness." Courtly Sir William was in his element. "And I am Sir William, escorted by Freddy the hamster." He hesitated. "Perhaps, Princess, you're surprised to find a tomcat in the company of a—"

"Not at all, Sir William. Nothing in the animal world surprises me. I used to be a sniffer dog, you see."

"Really?"

"Yes, I worked in customs. My job was to sniff out animal souvenirs. You've no idea the creatures people try to smuggle home with them, from snakes to centipedes."

"How immensely interesting, Princess."

118

CHARMING!

Time was running out, and His Lordship was making conversation with a princess. "Sir William," I whispered, "we must go and find Linda and Mr John."

"You're right, old boy." He leaned over and called down, "Your Highness, my companion has just pointed out that we're rather pressed for time. If I may be permitted to change the subject somewhat abruptly, have you by any chance seen two humans hereabouts?"

"A woman with red hair and a man with a big nose?"

"The very ones."

"My master did his job and asked them to leave. Politely, as is his way, but firmly."

"Hmm," said Sir William. Then: "Princess, may I ask you to do us a favour? Could you persuade your master to move on – politely but firmly?"

"With pleasure," said Princess Sonia, getting to her feet. She proceeded to bark and tug at her leash. The young man gave a start and said, "Quiet, Sonia!" But Sonia persisted, and he eventually stood up. "OK," he said, "let's take a look." And the two of them walked off.

Sir William climbed down. "Freddy, old boy, I doubt if there's much point in looking for Miss Carson and Mr John, not now."

He was right. There was only one possible course of action. "I must try to talk those hamsters into coming around," I said. I planned to start with Elvira. If I succeeded with her, as I hoped, the rest would fall into line. I gave Sir William the directions to Elvira's burrow, and he set off.

He'd taken precisely five steps when it happened.

The ground gave way beneath us! We fell through the earth and landed with a thud. There was a nasty metallic click, and everything went black.

Silence fell.

"Sir William," I said, "are you thinking what I'm thinking?"

"I don't know what *you're* thinking, old boy, but *I* think we're in a TRaP."

CHAPTER NINE

WE WERE SITTING in a steel-sided box embedded in the ground. The twin flaps on top were firmly secured by means of a spring lock. Someone had devised an extremely effective trap.

"But who, in the name of all that's sacred to cats?" Sir William sounded thoroughly irate. "And why?"

For the moment, nothing occurred to me either. Looking back, I can't quite understand why. My agitation was probably to blame. I'm only a hamster, after all. "We've got only one option, Sir William," I said. "When the trap is opened, you must leap out like a jack-in-the-box and make a run for it."

"An admirable plan, my dear fellow. Let's hope it works." Anxiously, Sir William added, "But if we're cooped up in here much longer, I wouldn't bet much on your cousins' chances."

Things could have been worse, though. After only ten

minutes we heard footsteps. Two humans were stealthily approaching.

Then someone spoke in a low voice. "Hey, Jake, this one's been sprung! There's something inside it."

"No real names, you dope!"

"OK, OK. Er, what was yours again?"

"It's time you remembered it: I'm Muskrat Two, and you're not Frank, you're Muskrat Three. Got that?"

Of course, the Muskrats! Great! We'd been trapped by animal conservationists.

"Sure," said Frank, "but there's no one around to hear us. Come on, help me lift it out." The trap was extracted from the ground. "Man, is it heavy! I didn't know field hamsters were such hulks. Should we take a peek at him?"

"What if he escapes? No, we'll take the trap to the other field and release him there."

"Hey, didn't Jenny say we've got to mark them first?"

"Jenny is Muskrat One! For heaven's sake, get that straight, Frank — er, Muskrat Three!"

"OK, OK, Jake – er, Muskrat Two. Well, what do we do now?"

"We go and see Muskrat One and ask her."

It was time for us to act. "Sir William," I said, "I think we should draw attention to ourselves."

"You really think they'd let us go, just like that?"

"**SHOOT!**" Jake said suddenly. "There are some construction workers coming! Quick, Frank, back to the car!"

And they hurried off carrying the trap between them. Uphill and down dale they ran, shaking us around like dice in a cup. Sir William mewed as loudly as he could, but the Muskrats were too preoccupied to notice.

They sprinted to their car as if ten Rottweilers of Princess Sonia's size were after them. The lid of the boot slammed shut, and off we went.

If my sense of direction didn't deceive me, we were making for the city. The Muskrats' car seemed to be pretty ancient, because it wheezed and rattled like mad. Sir William found the journey a terrible ordeal, especially after our cross-country dash.

"Freddy, my friend," he groaned, "I can't guarantee anything. Better keep out of the line of fire."

But he stuck it out, and he soon recovered once we got there and were carried out into the fresh air. "Freddy," he said, "I can't imagine what'll happen from now on, but I guess this puts an end to OPERATION JACK-IN-THE-BOX."

I had to agree with him. We would never make it back to the construction site, or only when it was far too late.

The two Muskrats carried us up a flight of stairs. A door opened and shut. Then they put our trap down.

"We're back, Muskrat One!"

"You can drop those stupid code names, Jake, at least

when we're here in the apartment." An attractive voice. Firm and clear, but pleasantly soft. When Jenny came over, she wafted a distinctive scent of rosemary into our prison. "Why did you bring that trap here? What's in there?"

"We haven't looked," said Frank.

"What *would* be in there?" Jake said, sounding miffed. "A hamster, of course."

"The animal kingdom is pretty diverse, or hadn't you heard? Aside from hamsters, it includes plenty of rabbits, weasels, and so on. The chances of there being a hamster in there are pretty remote, in my opinion. OK, open it."

There was a click, and the flaps were folded back.

There we sat: a huge black tomcat and a hamster on the small side. I mean, try to imagine what we looked like to humans confronted by such a twosome for the first time ever.

To begin with, the three of them just stood there in silence, staring.

"Well," Jake said after a while, "at least, I was fifty per cent right about the hamster."

"Except that it's not the kind of hamster we were expecting," said Jenny. She had short dark hair and a distinctive personal aroma — as I think I already mentioned — of rosemary. She eyed us closely. "A cat and a golden hamster, out there on the construction site . . . HMM. . ."

"I'm amazed," said Jake. "Normally, the cat would have eaten the hamster."

Quite so, my friend. As Jenny had observed, the animal kingdom is pretty diverse.

"Anyway," Frank said contentedly, "my trap worked like a charm."

"By the way, Jenny," said Jake, "the bulldozer is operating nights as well."

"Darn it, that complicates matters." Jenny thought for a moment. "OK, I think you'd better replace the trap and set it again. These two animals can stay here – it's too dangerous for them out there. But keep your eyes open. They weren't there by chance – they must belong to someone. And be careful."

"No need to tell *me* that, Muskrat One. Come on, Muskrat Three."

We were sitting on a blanket spread out on the floor near the sofa. Jenny had provided us with food (me with some grain and chopped apple, Sir William with meat from a can). She'd even dug out a cat's litter tray from somewhere, but Sir William loftily ignored it, at least for the time being.

"If only I knew what's up with you two," Jenny said,

regarding
us thoughtfully.
She had settled down
on the sofa with a book.
"And what am I to do with you?
I can't simply keep you." She sighed and
returned to her book. Its title was *Elementary Zoology*.

Before setting off, Jake and Frank had remembered why they'd brought the trap back in the first place: were the field hamsters to be marked? "No," Jenny decided after a moment's thought. "Handling them would stress them too much." Her book probably contained a chapter on hamster psychology.

"What do you think, Freddy?" Sir William said. "Will these Muskrats. . . Why 'Muskrats', anyway?"

"An interesting question, Sir William, but I don't have the answer."

"Pity. So what do you think? Will these Muskrats succeed in their efforts?"

"No," I said firmly. "No hamster in his right mind will venture out on to a field that's being flattened by a bulldozer. The only ones to end up in the Muskrats' traps will be you and me."

"So it's all up to us, as before. What's to be done?"

Sir William thought hard. I already knew what had to be done, but I didn't say so. I preferred the suggestion to come from Sir William himself. That meant I could cite him later on, when Mr John accused me of breaking my word.

"Freddy," said Sir William, "there's no alternative: you must make contact with these Muskrats."

Fine. All I had to do now was get Sir William to dispel my misgivings. "But," I said, "I promised Mr John, most faithfully, never to tell anyone I can read and write."

"Hmm," said Sir William. "True, but still. . ." He squared his shoulders. **"FREDDY, THIS IS AN EMERGENCY.**

You must make yourself known, but only to Jenny."

I'd already come to precisely the same conclusion.

"There's only one little snag," Sir William went on. He peered around. "I can't see a computer anywhere."

I hadn't spotted one either, but I'd been hoping my rather poor eyesight was to blame (sooner or later, I'm going to fix myself up with some glasses). "Sir William," I said, "Jenny is evidently studying zoology. She couldn't get by without a computer. There's got to be one somewhere in the apartment. Could you take a look around?"

"No problem, my dear fellow." Sir William rose and sauntered towards the door as unobtrusively as possible.

However, big black tomcats and unobtrusiveness don't go together. Jenny looked up. "Hey, cat!" she called. "Where are you off to?" She jumped off the sofa and shut the door. "Are you blind? Your toilet's over here."

"How could she be so gross!" Sir William exclaimed in Interanimal. He shook his head. "What now, old boy?"

I shrugged. "I know it sounds silly, but ONLY A MIRACLE CAN HELP US NOW."

The miracle took its time coming. All that happened was, Jake and Frank returned. "No luck," they reported. "Not a single hamster in any of the traps."

Jenny merely nodded. She had obviously realized the Muskrats' campaign was doomed to failure.

"We didn't see anyone either," Frank said. "Just a few construction workers."

"They didn't see *us*, though." Jake hesitated. Then he

said, "We'd better talk this over, Jenny. If they're working nights as well, I guess we'll have to resort to sabotage."

"Oh, sure," Jenny said sarcastically, "we'll blow up the bulldozer. Then we can take the hamsters quietly by the paw and escort them across to the other field."

"Nobody's talking about blowing anything up," said Jake. "But if we slipped some sugar into the bulldozer's gas tank, we'd gain some time."

"Yes, and bring another bulldozer and at least five more security guards hurrying to the scene." Angrily, Jenny ran her fingers through her hair. "This is stupid. Our e-mail to the news agency was stupid too — it's the only reason the construction site is guarded at this moment. I could kick myself for agreeing to send it."

"We'll never save those hamsters by playing softball."

"I think Jenny's right," said Frank.

"You would," said Jake. "That's because you don't have a mind of your own."

"Hey, don't give me that!"

"Cool it, cool it." Jenny stood up. "If we start

133

bickering among ourselves, we may as well forget the whole thing." She smiled. "Listen, how about a game? Just one round, OK?"

"Sure," said Frank. "It's been a while since we played."

"I'm in," said Jake.

Jenny fetched a box and they all sat down on the floor. "Usual rules," she said. "No foreign words, no proper names." The other two nodded. Then they started playing.

At first I didn't take much notice of what they were doing. Jenny wanted to create a friendly atmosphere, fair enough. But then I heard them say things like "Double letter score" and "Triple word score", and I pricked up my ears.

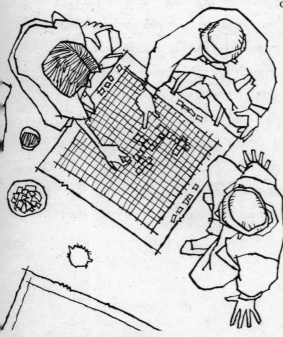

After a while I realized they were playing a game in which the object was to make words out of letters. Then I saw that the letters were printed on little wooden squares — pieces of wood so light, I could easily push them around myself. What was lying on the floor between the three of them was a method of writing that might have been specially designed for a hamster's paws!

i COULD MAKE CONTACT WITH JENNY!

With Jenny, who would probably keep my secret safe — yes, but Jake and Frank would discover it too. They seemed like nice enough fellows, but could I trust them with a secret? One that had to be kept at all costs?

No, I couldn't.

If I made myself known at this stage, I might endanger not only myself but others as well. Sophie, for instance.

I would have to keep quiet.

Just as I was turning away, it happened again:

"*Help! The Hamster Killer! Help!*"

CHAPTER TEN

THE CRY HAD THE SAME EFFECT on me as its predecessors. It made me jump to my feet in terror, fur bristling and teeth bared.

But something about this cry was new and altogether different.

It had come, not from some unknown source, but from a world with which I was now acquainted. It had been uttered by one of the field hamsters I'd seen assembled in the underground cavern – Jasper or Lulu, for example. I could tell that it hadn't come from Elvira.

And it carried a message: it told me I mustn't remain silent any longer.

Sir William had also sprung to his feet. "I can't pretend I'm getting used to these cries, my dear fellow." He glanced at the Muskrats, who were engrossed in their game, and sighed. "There are times when I wish I was as hard of hearing as a human." He looked at them more closely. "What are they doing?"

"Playing a game," I told him, "but a game that's now going to turn serious. Watch."

Keeping low to prevent any of the trio from spotting me too soon, I scampered over to them. I paused in the protective shelter of Jenny's feet and assessed the situation from my hiding place. There were at least twenty words criss-crossing one another on the board, and they included all the letters I needed! Jake was pondering his next move. OK, I told myself, this is it.

I darted out on to the board and swiftly shoved some letters together to spell FREDDY (a score of fourteen, incidentally – not bad for a beginner).

"Hey, it's my turn!" Jake protested. "Besides, proper names don't count. I thought we'd. . ." He broke off and stared down at me.

Jenny and Frank were also staring at me.

Next (breaking various rules of the game, I'm afraid) I spelled out THAT IS MY NAME.

Silence.

Then Frank said, "I must be going crazy. A hamster that can play Scrabble?"

"No," Jake said firmly, "a hamster that can spell."

"A hamster that can. . ." Jenny paused. Her eyes widened. "Tell me, er, Freddy – can you understand what we say?"

In order to spell the following answer I tipped the rest of the letters out of their bag. Then I wrote: YES JENNY I CAN UNDERSTAND YOU AND I CAN READ AND WRITE. It was quite a job pushing the requisite letters into position, of course, but I wanted to put to rest any doubts about my literacy and give the youngsters time to get used to the idea.

"Well," Jenny said at length, "I guess I can chuck my zoology book."

It took me only a quarter of an hour to fill in the Muskrats. This was because I was able to use Jenny's computer (there was one in the room next door, of course), and because I limited myself to essentials (Frank asked for a detailed account of how I'd learned to read and write, but I promised to tell him later). I also omitted certain facts (the cries for help in Interanimal, for example). It was simpler to say that we'd heard about the field hamsters through the agency report. In conclusion, I typed, *The hamsters must be moved to a different field as soon as possible.*

"That's just what we'd have done," said Jenny, "if we'd managed to trap them."

Sorry, I typed, *but it wouldn't have worked even then.*

"Why not?" asked Jake.

Because you can't relocate hamsters separately.

"But they're loners, aren't they?"

They are, I typed. *Each lives in its own burrow and wants nothing to do with the rest. But they all know one another — pretty well too. They have to, so they don't trespass on one another's territory. Field hamsters live alone but in a community. If you suddenly pluck them out of that community, they'll be so confused they'll get ill — or worse.*

"You mean," said Jenny, "that we can only resettle the whole colony at once, and only if they all agree?"

Correct.

"But we'll never manage it in one night, certainly not with a bulldozer churning around us."

"I told you!" Jake levelled his forefinger at Jenny. "We've got to buy time, stop the men working, and put their machines out of action!"

"Jake," Jenny said gently, "give us a break, would you?"

"OK." Jake folded his arms on his chest. "I can't wait to hear what *you* have in mind."

Frank raised a finger. "I think I've got it: the mayor

must ban all construction work until the hamsters are out of there."

"How are you going to persuade him to do that?" Jenny shook her head. "We can forget *that* idea."

"No, no," said Jake, "Frank's suggestion isn't as stupid as all that. The mayor must suspend the contractor's licence for a week, let's say. And how do we get him to do that?" He surveyed us with an air of triumph. "We kidnap him, and he stays kidnapped until he does what we want. Well, how about it?"

Jenny sighed. "For one brief moment I actually thought you had a sensible suggestion to make."

"OK, OK," said Jake, "I won't utter a word from now on. Still, the mayor would never dream of suspending the contractor's licence voluntarily."

And then I had an idea.

IT WAS a POSITIVELY BRILLIANT IDEa.

All right, I know, brilliant ideas don't come by themselves. Something happens or someone says something, and a brilliant idea pops into your head. I felt rather proud of myself for all that.

I know what to do, I typed. And I spelled out my plan on the screen.

"Terrific!" said Jake.

Frank nodded. "It might work."

"Provided the hamsters cooperate," said Jenny.

That was my plan's potential drawback. To be frank, the chances of persuading my cousins to go along with "Operation Mayor" were rather poor.

"Linda Carson? I'm Jenny of the Muskrats. . . That's right, I'm one of them. Er, Linda, somebody sends you

his best regards. It's Freddy." Linda's exclamation of delight could be heard all over the room.

Once we'd decided to adopt my scheme, the first step had been to write Linda's mobile phone number on the screen (I knew it by heart, needless to say) and Jenny dialled it. She told Linda what we were planning and arranged to rendezvous with her near the construction site. Then she hung up, looking slightly puzzled. "She sent her regards," she told me, "not only to you but also to someone called Sir William."

I indicated Sir William, who drew himself up to his full height.

"Oh," said Jenny, "so *you're* Sir William. I hope I wasn't rude to you earlier."

Sir William mewed with old-world courtesy and permitted himself to be stroked.

Then it was time to drive to the construction site. Feeling genuinely sorry for Sir William as we got back into the car, I expressed my sympathy.

"Thanks, old boy," he said. With a grim smile, he added, "I've borne this ordeal twice, so why not bear it thrice?"

Oh dear, Sir William was becoming a rhymester too. Was that what they call gallows humour? In view of its quality, I could only hope that this would be his first and last attempt at verse.

But Sir William survived this trip too, without disgracing himself. When the Muskrats' car turned off along a track through the wood and pulled up shortly afterwards, he even announced, "D'you know, Freddy, I think I'm becoming accustomed to car travel."

Although it was dark by now, the Muskrats didn't take long to find Linda and Mr John, who had been waiting for them and were highly relieved to be reunited

with
me and Sir
William. A brief
commotion followed as the
humans introduced themselves. Then we
all set off for the construction site.

We could hear the bulldozer rumbling and squeaking a long way off. This time, since Sir William was feeling so chipper, I travelled sitting on the back of his neck. I could see almost nothing in the darkness of the wood. To Sir William, on the other hand, it might have been daylight, he padded along so sure-footedly.

After a while he said, "The light's growing stronger, Freddy. There's something going on in the hamsters' field. We should warn our friends to be careful."

"But how?" I asked, because Linda hadn't turned on

her laptop yet. "I think they'll be sufficiently careful without being warned, Sir William."

However, it wasn't until we were quite close to the field that the humans smelled a rat. Mr John came to a halt.

"Something's up," he said.

"You're right," said Frank, "there's a lot of light over there."

It grew lighter and lighter. Stealthily, we made our way to the edge of the wood bordering the hamsters' field and peered through the undergrowth.

"Oh, no!" said Jenny.

The field was brilliantly illuminated.

CHAPTER ELEVEN

THREE FLOODLIGHTS HAD BEEN ERECTED on poles. One of them was some way off, near where the bulldozer was trundling to and fro, but the other two illuminated the expanse in front of us as bright as day.

Two men in construction workers' helmets were walking across the field, each carrying a metal box.

"Hey!" Frank blurted out. "That's two of our traps they've found."

"And the others are lying on the edge of the field," said Jake. "Oh well, so the whole idea was a flop. It doesn't matter."

"What does matter is those lights." Jenny shook her head. "We can't launch Operation Mayor like this."

"Certainly not right now," said Linda. "Look, there's a security guard coming."

"We'd better make ourselves scarce," said Mr John.

With him in the lead, we withdrew a short distance into the wood.

"What do you think, Sir William?" I asked.

"I think the same as you, old boy."

Sir William pawed at Mr John's trouser leg. Mr John caught on at once and asked Linda to turn on her laptop.

Wait here, I typed. *We're going to have a word with the guard dog.*

I just had time, as Sir William bounded off with me aboard, to hear Jenny say, "They're going to speak to the dog? But how? As far as I know, cats and hamsters can't bark." It probably wouldn't be long before she not only chucked her zoology book but abandoned college altogether.

The young security guard in the black uniform had paused on the edge of the wood and was watching the two construction workers as

148

they continued to comb the field for more traps. Beside him stood Princess Sonia.

"Good evening, Sir William," she said. She had probably scented us when we were still deep inside the woods. "Delighted to see you again."

"The pleasure is all mine, Your Highness." Sir William was master of the situation once more. "I should so much like to meet with you sometime on a purely social level, Princess, but I fear that a matter of some urgency renders it desirable for me to—"

"I know," said Princess Sonia. "You want to rescue those hamsters."

Sir William's jaw dropped. "You know?"

"Of course, one scents all kinds of things. I'm bound to say that I don't have much time for greedy rodents—

149

present company excluded – but exterminating them is going a bit too far. Is there anything I can do to help?"

"Indeed there is, Princess. You can persuade that man beside you——"

"Eddy."

"Huh?"

"My master's name is Eddy. I only mention that, Sir William, to dispel the impression that he's just any old security guard. Eddy is my master, and a good master too."

"But of course, Princess, I'm sure he is." Sir William cleared his throat. "The thing is, we'd like you to distract your master's attention for a while, and also, if possible, get him to turn off those awful lights."

"Hmm," said Princess Sonia, "I don't think that's beyond the bounds of possibility. The suggestion will have to come from a human, of course. A human my master takes to at once – best of all a human female. But not," she added, "the lady with the red hair."

I had meant to leave negotiations entirely to Sir

William, but I couldn't stop myself. "Why not?" I demanded.

"I don't care for her perfume."

"NOW LISTEN," I began, but Sir William cut in.

"I think we can produce someone else, Princess."

"Good." Princess Sonia sat down. "In that case, Sir William, let's agree on a rendezvous."

We had withdrawn to a small clearing somewhat deeper in the woods and concealed ourselves in the surrounding undergrowth. (That applied mainly to the humans, of course. A small rodent and a pure black tomcat have little trouble concealing themselves in a dark forest.)

It wasn't long before Princess Sonia came panting into view, towing Eddy behind her on the leash. He was armed with a big torch.

In the middle of the clearing she paused and sat down.

"Oh, so this is the place you meant." Eddy shone the beam of the torch this way and that. "Anyone there?" he called.

He listened a while, then shook his head. "Nothing. What's the matter with you, Sonia? This is the second time today you've taken me on a wild-goose chase." He turned to go. "Come along."

But Princess Sonia didn't budge.

"Hmm," said Eddy. He switched off his torch and listened.

There was a sudden rustle behind him.

Eddy spun around, switched on the torch – and there she stood.

That's to say, she didn't just stand there; she materialized in the beam of light like an otherworldly apparition.

Eddy stared at her.

"Hi there," said the apparition.

"H-hello," stammered Eddy.

Then the apparition smiled a sweet, otherworldly smile and said, "I'm Jenny, who are you?"

Jenny's meeting with Eddy proved a total success from every angle. The two of them strolled off out of earshot (Jake registered this with a snort of disapproval). When Jenny returned a few minutes later she was able to report that Eddy (they were evidently on first-name terms) would not only turn a blind eye to our activities but was thoroughly in sympathy with them.

"He's got a soft spot for hamsters," she said, "and he's quite OK in other respects as well." Jake declared that anyone on the payroll of people who murdered hamsters couldn't possibly be "OK". Jenny angrily retorted that (a) Eddy was not paid by the mayor or the construction company and (b) that Jake was talking absolute junk. Jake was about to make some furious rebuttal when Mr

John stepped in and asked whether the floodlights would be turned off.

"Yes," said Jenny. "Eddy says he'll give the order. He's bound to get into trouble, but he's prepared to risk that."

It was some time before the floodlights actually went out and Sir William could sprint off across the field with me guiding him from my perch on his back. Our objective was the exit tunnel of Elvira's burrow. Several hours had elapsed since we'd left Enrico and Caruso behind. I dreaded to think what the field hamsters had done to them. Or vice versa.

The course I'd set for the exit tunnel proved accurate to the nearest inch (I'll refrain from priding myself on this feat of orientation). When we got there, Sir William said, "I'd appreciate it if you could emerge from the same hole this time, old boy."

"You won't have any trouble seeing me, Sir William," I told him. "Either I won't emerge at all because I'll have met my end down there, or you'll spot me with ease because I'll have a whole tribe of field hamsters with me."

Sir William nodded. "In that case, Freddy, the best of luck."

"Thanks," I said and re-entered the realm of the field hamsters.

The tunnel was pitch-black, but a hamster's whiskers enable him to find his way in the dark as unerringly as a bat's radar (OK, OK, almost as unerringly). The smell pattern, which also helped me to get my bearings, told me that Elvira was not in her burrow.

Instead of Elvira's scent I picked up another –

a scent i knew only too well.

It grew steadily stronger the nearer I got to her living quarters. I rounded a bend in the tunnel, and there, by the phosphorescent light of a piece of rotting wood, I saw them.

They were sitting there with their heads bowed, all hunched up and looking thoroughly disconsolate. There

was no doubt about it: Enrico and Caruso were in the depths of despair. It was a sight that gladdened my heart.

Before my readers accuse me of being heartless, I should like to draw attention to certain facts. First, I had a pretty tough job ahead of me. Egged on by their priest, these ferocious field hamsters were determined not to be

156

rescued. Not only did I have to win them over, I had to spur them into action. Second, my paws were raw, and I was faced with another long and arduous trek to the cavern containing the Jar of Hope. In short, the last thing I needed just then was a pair of buffoons intent on bugging me with their tasteless wisecracks.

"Hello, you guys," I said.

"Freddy!" Enrico positively beamed.

"THaNK HeaVeNS YOU'Re HeRe aT LaST!" Caruso threw up his paws in delight.

At that particular moment I felt a touch of genuine sympathy for them, I won't deny.

"It's awful," Enrico reported. "We've never seen such a depressed bunch of field hamsters. Even Elvira's feeling down in the mouth."

"We wanted to cheer them up a bit," said Caruso, "so we devised an amusing skit with a bulldozer in it."

"To rob the thing of its terrors," said Enrico, "if you know what I mean. I played the driver and Caruso the bulldozer."

157

"My most difficult role to date," Caruso put in modestly.

"But they BOOED us off the stage!" said Enrico.

"And chased us out of the cave!" Caruso added.

I clicked my tongue in commiseration, secretly congratulating my cousins on their good taste. "So they're all assembled in the cavern with the jar in it?"

"Yes, Fronso is planning to hold another Banquet of Hope."

"When?"

"If we hurry, we should just get there in time."

I'll spare my readers a description of the long trek that followed. It's enough to say, I was on my last legs by the time we reached our destination.

I'd caught the sound of Fronso's penetrating voice from deep inside the tunnel. When I finally peeked out into the cavern, the obese little brute had just finished his sermon. He raised both paws.

"LET US PRAY."

The hamsters turned to face the centre of the underground chamber. As before, they were sitting well spaced out.

"O Jar of Hope!" Fronso intoned. "Unto thee we lift up our eyes. Hear us! Look upon this great abundance of sacrificial offerings and be gracious unto us."

He wasn't exaggerating. Lying in mounds at the foot of the jar was at least twice as much grain as before. If the hamsters had voluntarily parted with such vast quantities of food, they must have been really depressed.

"In thee, noble Jar," Fronso boomed, "repose our dearest hopes. Thy precious contents will not fail us."

"Thy precious contents will not fail us," chorused the hamsters. They fixed the jar with a despairing, yearning gaze.

"Partake, therefore, of the Banquet of Hope!"

"We partake of the Banquet of Hope," they chanted.

Even as they did so, gazing longingly at the jar, an idea occurred to me.

I'll refrain from describing it as brilliant (although I

160

believe it was) because I might be thought conceited. But when I explained my plan in a whisper to Enrico and Caruso, who were hunkered down just behind me, their reaction was quite spontaneous: "What a simply brilliant idea!"

Meanwhile, the hamsters had raised their voices in song:

"Jar of Hope, to thee we pray,
we will ne'er thy trust betray.
May we ever rue the day
if we fail our dues to pay."

"Beloved hamsters of the field!" Fronso intoned. "This time, thanks to your abundant offerings, the Jar of Hope will assuredly grant our prayer."

That was when I bounded out into the cavern and cried, **"YOUR PRIEST IS A FRAUD!"**

CHAPTER TWELVE

ALL THE HAMSTERS SWUNG around with a jerk. It took them a moment to grasp who I was. A very brief moment.

"It's the pygmy hamster!" someone cried.

A hissing snarl went up from the congregation. It wasn't particularly loud, but it was so sharp, it almost cut me in two. At this point, I strongly doubted whether we would succeed, but I yelled, "Now!"

Enrico and Caruso came dashing out of the mouth of the tunnel. You couldn't really call it "dashing", of course, but they certainly moved faster than I'd have given a guinea pig credit for. They scuttled through the congregation to the pedestal and climbed it in no time. Then – I held my breath because I genuinely didn't know if they were strong enough – they seized the jar by the handles and tipped it over.

They had overturned the Jar of Hope!

It fell off the pedestal and landed on the floor of the cavern, losing its lid in the process. It rolled a little way, then came to a stop with its mouth facing the congregation.

They could all see inside it.

Silence, then: "BUT it'S EMPTY!"

It was only an isolated cry, but so filled with disappointment, so fraught with rage, that it shook me. The hamsters started shouting. "Where are all the maggots? Where are all our offerings? Where's all our grain?" they bellowed.

"Hamsters of the field!" Fronso was standing on his pedestal with his paws raised, trying to make himself heard. "Hamsters of the field!" he yelled again. "Listen to me!"

The hamsters fell silent.

Surveying the congregation, I realized that this was

the moment of truth. Fronso might well turn the tables on us.

"Hamsters of the field!" cried Fronso. "Does it really surprise you that the Jar of Hope is empty?"

The hamsters gazed at him expectantly, whiskers twitching.

"Of course it's empty!" cried Fronso. "Of course there's nothing inside it! Why not?" He paused for effect. "Because you can't see hopes! Hopes are invisible!"

Quite right, Fronso, but there are situations in which the right thing can be completely wrong.

"Hamsters of the field! Don't be deceived!"

That was Elvira.

Towering over the congregation, she boomed, "There never was anything in the jar. No hopes – nothing! That jar has never been anything but empty! Do you want to know where our offerings went to? Do you want to know what happened to our grain?" She looked around. "All our offerings, all our grain – Fronso nicked it all!"

The silence lasted long enough for the hamsters to absorb this information, but no longer. Then a snarl of rage went up. It seemed to issue from a single throat and made the air in the cavern tremble.

The hamsters began to converge from all sides, slowly but with grim determination.

Fronso was crouching motionless on his pedestal. He crouched there as if rooted to the spot, his eyes wide with mortal terror as he watched the advancing congregation.

The ring around him tightened.

Then it happened again.

Only a tremor at first, it quickly developed into an earthquake that shook the cavern so hard, clods of soil began to fall from the roof. The bulldozer was passing overhead!

The hamsters stared up at the roof in horror. Suddenly, someone yelled, "Hey, the priest!"

Fronso was just disappearing, nimble as a pygmy hamster, down one of the side tunnels.

"After him!"

"No, stop!" shouted Elvira. "Stay here!"

The hamsters stopped short.

"We must save ourselves!" Elvira roared. "Fronso doesn't matter."

The earthquake was swiftly subsiding. "Curse you, Elvira!" cried a female hamster. "It'll be your fault if that swindler gives us the slip!"

"Forget about the miserable wretch, Lulu," Elvira retorted. "We must concentrate all our efforts on saving ourselves from the Hamster Killer."

"Elvira's right," said a male hamster. "Let Fronso go."

"Sure, Jasper," sneered Lulu, "that's just what I'd have expected you to say, you wimp!"

"Take that back at once!" yelled Jasper.

"**STOP IT!**" snapped Elvira. "Squabbling will get us nowhere."

"Butt out, Elvira," said another female hamster. "What gives you the right to order us around?"

"I can tell you the answer to that, Dolores," said yet another hamster. "It's because she's got a whole heap more sense than you, for instance."

"Oh," snarled Dolores, "so you're sticking your paw in too, are you? Clean out your burrow first, Denzil, I can smell it from mine."

I'd been listening open-mouthed. I knew my cousins weren't the most easy-going of rodents, but this display of bad temper was getting on my nerves. If they all went for one another now, we could say goodbye to Operation Mayor. I raced to the pedestal as fast as I could and sat up on my haunches. "Hamsters of the field!" I cried at the top of my voice.

They all turned towards me.

"My dear cousins. . ." I surveyed the assembled hamsters, all of whom were two or three times my size.

"First, I'd like to set the record straight, once and for all: I'm not a pygmy hamster." I drew myself up to my full height. "I'm a golden hamster."

An amused murmur made itself heard. Many of the field hamsters smirked, others actually laughed. What on earth had I said that was so funny? Bewildered, I looked across at Elvira. She was chuckling too.

"Freddy," she boomed, "it doesn't matter two hoots whether you're a pygmy hamster, a golden hamster, or even a field hamster. You're our cousin from the city, and you've unmasked Fronso at last – with the aid of your two courageous friends." She pointed to Enrico and Caruso, who were still sitting on the pedestal recently occupied by the Jar of Hope. They rose and bowed in all directions before blowing Elvira kisses.

She smiled at their flattery. Then she turned serious again. "Above all, Freddy, you're the one who knows how we can save ourselves."

My cousins nodded.

"If I may put in a word here," said Denzil, raising his paw. "Cousin Freddy already told us how: we must leave this field."

"That's right," said Elvira, "but without that lousy old jar."

General laughter.

"Without the jar," said Denzil, "but complete with our stores. Harvest time is nearly over, and I wouldn't find it particularly amusing to escape the Hamster Killer only to die of starvation."

Quite so. Cousin Denzil had put his paw on the point I wanted to get at. "Of course, you must take your stores with you," I said. "We'll fix that, but there are many other arrangements to be made. For example, your new field must be chosen with care, so you're not driven out again. And what does that mean?" I scanned my audience. "It means we need more time."

Everyone nodded.

"So we must *make* more time," I went on. "We must compel the Hamster Killer to suspend operations until you've moved into your new home. And now I'll tell you how we're going to do that."

I paused. Now came the hardest part of my task: how to render Operation Mayor acceptable to my newfound cousins. It meant hitting them hard right at the start. **WHY?** Because the first phase of my plan entailed taking them all for a ride in a car.

I mean, put yourself in their position. Unlike us golden hamsters, who inhabit a modern, technological world (we all have tread-wheels in our cages, if not carousels), field hamsters never come into direct contact with anything more technological than a farm tractor.

They dwell in underground burrows and harvest their grain in entirely natural surroundings.

And these were the children of nature whom I was supposed to talk into an adventurous journey by car!

They all stared at me expectantly.

I began as cautiously as I could. "The first time I was here, I told you what a car or automobile was."

"Yes," said Dolores. "It's a box on wheels in which humans travel – a kind of passenger tractor."

"Precisely," I said. "And a passenger tractor is a very practical means of getting to somewhere far away. So far away you can't make it on foot."

The hamsters nodded, but I could sense they were growing uneasy. My task seemed to be getting even harder than I'd thought. I would have to tread more carefully still.

"Humans think nothing of travelling by car – I mean, by passenger tractor. Most animals don't either. I myself have done so several times, and I can assure you there's nothing to it."

I saw Jasper and Dolores exchange looks and decided to shift down another gear. "The thing is, anyone seeing a passenger tractor for the first time may possibly feel a bit scared." I cleared my throat. "I can imagine that some of you would feel the same. Well, er. . ."

They were all staring at me.

"Well," I went on, "I'll have to come out with it sometime: could you envision the possibility – you yourselves, I mean. . ."

They continued to stare.

"You mean," said Jasper, his eyes widening, "that we're going for a ride in a passenger tractor?"

I could only nod.

"Wow!" said Dolores. She heaved a deep, contented sigh. "We've always dreamed of going for a tractor ride."

CHAPTER THIRTEEN

SIR WILLIAM AND I WERE AGAIN seated on the shelf at the rear of Linda's car. So, to my regret, were Enrico and Caruso.

All the field hamsters had climbed – or rather, been lifted – aboard the Muskrats' car. In the first place, because there was plenty of room for them, and, second, because Sir William had put his foot down hard (more of that later).

My prediction had proved correct. Sir William had quickly spotted me, the guinea pigs and the colony of field hamsters, even though we emerged a long way from Elvira's burrow. Although I'd naturally warned my cousins what to expect, they were rather dismayed by the sudden appearance of a huge black tomcat. However, Sir William defused the situation with a few courteous remarks that went over well, especially with the lady hamsters.

174

With Sir William in the lead, we proceeded to the edge of the woods, where our human friends were waiting.

I'd told the hamsters about them as well — in considerable detail — but the unfamiliar presence of humans scared them so much, they were on the point of running back across the field in a blind panic. Then Jenny started talking. I can't recall what she said, but it didn't matter, the sound of her clear, melodious voice stopped my cousins in their tracks. Then they caught her delightful scent of rosemary, and that clinched it: Jenny had won them over. They remained mistrustful of the other humans, but with Jenny around nothing could alarm them from then on.

Our friends had parked their cars as near to the field as they dared. Once the hamsters had got over their mild disappointment (the cars did not entirely correspond to their notion of "passenger tractors"), they addressed the question of who was to travel with whom.

"I wouldn't ride in the same car as Lulu," Jasper announced, "– not for all the grain the the world!"

"At least we're in agreement for once," Lulu said venomously.

"And I can't sit with Denzil for health reasons," said Dolores.

"What health reasons?"

"You smell so bad, it's enough to make one ill."

"I'll make you ill, all right!" snapped Denzil. "Just you wait!"

"Hey," Elvira cut in, "do me a favour and stop bickering."

Dolores rounded on her. "What's it to you? Just because a pair of guinea pigs pay court to you, I suppose you think you're royalty!"

"Envy, thy name is Dolores," sneered Denzil.

"Shut up a moment," said another female hamster. "I

want to make one thing clear: I don't mind sitting with Elvira, but not with Lulu."

"You don't imagine I want to sit with *you*, do you?" snarled Lulu. "You and your slovenly fur-cleaning habits! You're a—"

"Please, ladies, please!" exclaimed Sir William. "Gentlemen too! You're all getting worked up unnecessarily. The limited space in Miss Carson's automobile is reserved for permanent staff. You field hamsters will all be travelling in the other one."

Our trip in Linda's car began harmoniously enough. Enrico and Caruso kept quiet and behaved themselves, and Sir William felt confident that he'd conquered his car sickness.

But then it attacked him again – **AND HOW!**

"Friends," he groaned, "I think I'm going to be. . ." And he was.

"Oh, dear," he said, when he'd more or less got his breath back, "how terribly embarrassing, and in dear

Miss Carson's car, of all places. I hope she'll forgive me." He paused. "I'm still feeling nauseous too."

"We could make you feel better, Sir William," Enrico volunteered.

"Yes," said Caruso, "we did you good the last time."

"Boys," I said hastily, "I think the best thing for Sir William would be a little peace and quiet."

Sir William gave a faint smile. "I'm really touched by your concern, Freddy, but I do believe a spot of humour might do the trick." He turned to Enrico and Caruso. "What did you have in mind?"

Heaven help you if it's a joke at my expense, I thought. Not even Sir William can save you this time.

"We've got a skit for you," said Enrico. "It's called 'The Third Man.'"

"It's very funny, honestly," said Caruso.

"Excellent," Sir William said eagerly. "Please proceed."

But Enrico shook his head sadly. "No can do."

"Why not?"

"Because there's only two of us," Caruso explained.

"The Third Man wouldn't have to do much," said Enrico.

They were looking at me.

"Just a minute!" I exclaimed. "You mean me? NO, NOT ON YOUR LiFE."

"Please, Freddy," Enrico begged. "Be a sport. All you'd have to do is lose your temper. Surely you could manage that?"

"No, I couldn't. Forget it."

"You'd only have to pretend," said Caruso.

"I realize that," I snapped, "but all the same, you're wasting your time."

They exchanged mournful glances. "But the skit will only work with three characters," Enrico said plaintively.

"If you can't manage with two, you'll have to abandon the idea." I was getting hot under the collar by now. "Drop it. The matter's closed. FINITO!"

"Enrico," Caruso said sorrowfully, "I do believe he really doesn't want to."

181

"Please, Freddy!" Enrico clasped his paws together.

"For the umpteenth time, no!" I yelled. "I refuse to play the Third Man for you! I won't do it, I tell you!"

"You spoke too soon, old boy," said Sir William. "Or too late, depending on one's point of view."

"What? Er, what do you mean?"

But Sir William didn't reply. He merely grinned from ear to ear, and Enrico and Caruso broke into song:

"We roar with laughter when we see
a blind cow seek its hay in vain,
or when a blind hen by mistake
pecks up some dust instead of grain,
or when a blind man gropes his way
along, then trips and has a fall.
But oh, a hamster blind with rage
we find the funniest sight of all."

And they howled with mirth in a shameless display of malicious glee.

I yearned to bite them – itched to sink my razor-sharp teeth into their flesh! With a superhamsterish effort I remained sitting there, outwardly calm and composed. I even managed to prevent my fur from bristling. OK, OK, so they'd tricked me yet again – with my active assistance, I had to admit. I decided to put the matter on hold.

Sir William, who had been watching me, nodded approvingly.

As he saw it, I'd behaved like a civilized domestic animal.

One thing was certain: my trip through space to the sinister being in GaLaXY999 was as good as booked.

We didn't park the cars right outside the entrance, needless to say. Linda, who was directing Operation Mayor with Mr John's assistance, had picked a suitable spot on the street map. It was far enough from the mayor's house to avoid arousing suspicion, but near enough for us animals to cover the distance on foot without exhausting ourselves.

On our first visit to interview the mayor, Mr John had gathered that there was a rear entrance accessible from the backyard.

We headed in that direction.

Each of us knew exactly what to do.

Before we set off, Mr John conducted a final run-through (I know that's what always happens in mediocre heist movies, but it's the right thing to do).

"Your job, Sir William?" asked Mr John.

I keyed his answer into Linda's laptop. *Responsible for Freddy's transportation and also for reconnoitring the route.*

Mr John nodded. "Enrico and Caruso?"

Keep watch on the backyard gate. In the event of danger: two shrill whistles.

"Jake?"

"Watch the front entrance. Danger signal: one shrill whistle."

"Frank?"

"Pick the lock on the back door."

"Jenny?"

"Escort the team to the bedroom door and open it."

"Good," said Mr John. "Then Freddy and his friends will go into action." He shrugged his shoulders. "After that we'll simply have to trust our luck – the luck every worthy cause deserves."

It was long past midnight when we reached the mayor's backyard gate, where we left Enrico and Caruso on guard. Linda and Mr John had already left. The rest of us stole cautiously up to the back door. Everything now depended on how it was secured.

"Opening it won't be the problem," Frank had said at our preliminary discussion. "I can pick any lock as long as it isn't a high-security job. The problem is closing it again. Nobody must know we were ever there."

In fact, he got the door open in less than a minute (using a tool that grated terribly on our sensitive ears). "We're in luck," he whispered. "It was a breeze. When you leave, just pull it shut, OK? Good hunting."

We made our way cautiously inside. I took the lead on Sir William's back, followed by the field hamsters and Jenny.

I checked the smell pattern. "His bedroom is upstairs on the second floor," I whispered. I could have located that pipe smoker even in a stinking pigsty.

Unlike us hamsters and Jenny, Sir William could easily make

out the stairs in the darkness. The field hamsters found climbing them them somewhat difficult, but they managed it in a surprisingly short time

by scrambling on to one another's backs. We came to a halt outside the bedroom door. With infinite care, Jenny turned the handle and opened it.

"Good luck," she whispered, and we animals tiptoed in.

THEN CAME THE REALLY HARD PART.

I mean, try to picture the situation. A big black tomcat and a score of rodents had invaded a bedroom completely unfamiliar to them. Sir William would be concealing himself beneath the bed, but it was different for us hamsters. We had to take up positions where we would be clearly visible but within easy reach of hiding places to which we could retreat in a flash when the time came.

Of course, we'd debated what to do if things failed to turn out as we hoped. The result of our deliberations was pretty depressing – so much so that Mr John had said, "Kids, you've got no choice. This simply has to work."

Sir William halted at the foot of the bed. "Freddy, my friend," he whispered, "I'm going to arch my back. See if you can climb on to the bed."

"OK," I whispered when I was safely there. "You go and hide."

I waited a while in the darkness, then broadcast a question in Interanimal: "Is everyone in position?"

There was no reply, but that was the prearranged signal meaning **"READY!"**

Now it was up to me.

I'd been wondering which part of the body would be most suitable. Big toe? Finger? Earlobe? No, I had a better idea.

Slowly, I sidled along the huge, snoring body.

Until I reached my destination.

I concentrated hard, then rose on my haunches

AND BIT.

Quick as a flash, I hid behind the pillow.

The mayor sat up with a positively inhuman scream.

Silence fell. After a while, he groaned and started to pant. Then I heard him grope for the light switch.

The light came on.

The mayor sat there, breathing heavily and staring into space. All at once he stiffened.

He had spotted the first hamster.

It was sitting on a low chest at the foot of the bed. The mayor stared at it; the hamster stared back. Then it reared up and snarled.

More snarls made themselves heard on all sides. The mayor surveyed the room in horror. There were hamsters wherever he looked: on the chest of drawers, on his pipe rack, on the bookshelves, on the rolltop desk in the corner. There were even hamsters on the bedside table. And all of them had blown out their cheek pouches and bared their teeth in a snarl.

There was a knock at the door. "Mr Mayor? Are you all right?"

"Martha!" The mayor jumped out of bed and ran to the door in his baggy pajamas. He wrenched it open and dashed out into the hallway. "Martha," we heard him say, "thank God you're here! I mean, good of you to be so concerned." He hesitated. "Would you mind, er, taking a look in my room? I thought I saw something, er, unusual. . ."

"Hide!" I hissed, but the hamsters had already taken cover.

Big, bony Martha marched into the bedroom and looked around. "Looks fine to me," she declared.

The mayor poked his head around the door. "No hamsters?"

"Hamsters? Oh, I get it." Martha put her hands on her hips. "You were dreaming of hamsters, eh? Because of that business with the automobile plant. Am I right?"

The mayor nodded. "But it was so realistic. An absolute nightmare."

"In that case, sir," said Martha, "take care your nightmare doesn't become a habit."

She left the room and the mayor got back into bed. He sighed, plumped up his pillow (I'd naturally secreted myself in the crack between the headboard and the mattress), and turned out the light.

It took him roughly ten minutes to drop off again.

I waited another five minutes. Then, when his breathing sounded reassuringly peaceful, I broadcast another message into the darkness: "Attention! Get ready!"

I waited a little longer. I'd originally thought of biting him in a different place the second time, but the first bite had proved so effective, I saw no reason to change my tactics. The result proved me right.

The mayor sat up with another inhuman scream, but this time he turned on the light at once. He looked around wildly, and there they were again.

Snarling, menacing hamsters wherever he looked.

"Martha!" He dashed out of the room, and we heard him hammering on a door along the passage. "Martha! Where are my sleeping tablets?"

"Yes, yes, calm down, I'll make you a nice mug of hot milk. Come along, sir."

They started down the stairs.

"But I'll guarantee you one thing," I heard Martha say. "You won't get rid of that nightmare of yours with hot milk and sleeping tablets. You'll have to think of something else."

CHAPTER FOURTEEN

I WAS BACK IN MY CAGE some hours later.

I'd just finished grooming my fur (a process as important to us hamsters as cleaning their teeth is to humans) and was about to retire to my nest, intending to curl up and sleep until dinnertime. I would have done that in any case, but after last night's exertions sleep was doubly necessary.

"Hello?" The phone had rung. "Hi, Linda. At work already?"

Of course, today was Linda's first day at the local TV station. After a sleepless night too! She must have driven straight there after dropping us at Mr John's.

"Really? Congratulations! When? . . . So soon? Great, I can hardly wait! Bye." Mr John hung up. "Kids!" he called. "Rendezvous in front of the TV at seven o'clock sharp. Then we'll find out whether or not Operation Mayor was successful."

When the mayor and Martha had disappeared downstairs, I was confronted by a knotty problem: should we repeat the procedure or leave it at that?

What argued in favour of repeating the procedure was that, after the hamster brigade's third or fourth appearance, the mayor would probably go to any lengths to get rid of his nightmare. Another advantage, to be honest, was that tormenting him gave me a great big kick.

On the other hand, while the mayor and Martha were downstairs we could slip away without difficulty. If we stayed and were discovered, all would be lost.

What was it Great-Grandmother used to say? "NO ONE CAN SNEAK THE FOOD IN YOUR CHEEK."

Well, the food in our cheeks would have to suffice. I gave the order to withdraw. We did so without incident (discounting the fact that we'd hardly reached the backyard gate when my beloved cousins got into an argument over which of them had snarled the loudest).

We suggested transporting them to a temporary place of safety, but they firmly rejected this idea – unanimously, for once. They had been away from their field for far too long, they said, and were feeling thoroughly homesick. So we took them back, and they disappeared into their burrows. We could only hope they came to no harm, because everything still hung in the balance.

What, we wondered, if "the food in our cheeks" hadn't been enough?

We assembled in front of the TV just before seven. Mr John sat on the sofa, and we animals watched from the coffee table (over which Mr John had draped an old woollen blanket, presumably to protect it from Enrico's and Caruso's unsanitary habits).

The programme, which started on time, was called *Off the Cuff,* and the host was a young man whose pudgy face beamed as if he'd been looking forward to this moment all night long. "Good morning all!" he began. "'We shed light on what happened last night' – that's the motto of our programme, in which a person in authority comments off the cuff on some important event that occurred during the night."

The picture on the screen split into two to reveal Linda as well as the young man. "And now," he cried, "it's my pleasure to welcome our new reporter, Linda Carson. Hello there, Linda! Whose off-the-cuff comments have you managed to obtain for us this morning?"

"Hello there, Stephen," said Linda, who was holding a fat microphone. The young man disappeared, and she now filled the entire screen. "Today," she went on, "the person who has kindly consented to be interviewed is" – she turned her head, and the camera followed her gaze – "the mayor of our great city."

The mayor was lolling back in the roomy leather armchair behind his desk. His smile was as amiable and sincere as only the smile of a man with nothing to hide can be.

But there was a minor problem. The mayor wasn't looking his best – far from it. Not to mince matters, he looked a regular sight – like a small-time crook who'd got mixed up in a street fight. Adhered crosswise to his bulbous nose were two big Band-Aids.

What was the advice with which Great-Grandmother had dispatched us youngsters on our journey through life? "Remember, my dears: be kind and be good, but, if you must bite, be sure to draw blood."

"Your Honour," said Linda, "you're planning to build a new automobile plant on a site believed to be occupied by field hamsters. Field hamsters are a strictly protected species. You should never have approved the scheme. Why, then, is the plant being built?"

"Why? Because experts have ascertained that no hamsters are living there." The mayor leaned forward.

198

"I'm glad, Miss Carson, that you, in your, er, new capacity, should be so anxious to give the public a true picture of the situation."

"Are there really no hamsters on the site?"

"I assure you there aren't." The TV screen was now showing the mayor in close-up. He gazed at the camera with a cordial smile, seemingly untroubled by the Band-Aids on his nose. "I give you my word."

That was that.

We stared at one another in dismay. It had all been in vain.

Sir William looked positively miserable, Enrico and Caruso were hanging their heads in a pathetic manner, and Mr John was breathing hard. As for me, I felt so wretched I could have crept away and hidden in my nest.

My cousins the field hamsters — Elvira, Jasper, Lulu, Denzil, Dolores and the rest — were past saving.

"So everything's on the up-and-up," we heard Linda say. She paused for a moment. "In that case, Your Honour," she said abruptly, "why were some hamster traps installed on the construction site? And why, Your Honour, were they removed last night in the course of a cloak-and-dagger operation?"

The mayor stared at her. "How did you know about that?"

"I know it, that's all. So why?"

"I'll, er, be glad to tell you." The mayor paused and fingered the Band-Aids on his nose. Apparently, he felt they might be coming unstuck, and it took him quite some time to make sure that this was not the case. "As far as the events of last night are concerned —" he began, only to break off once more. He wrinkled his nose, rubbed it gingerly, screwed up his face, and then. . . Out it came, a sneeze as explosive as a firecracker. Not just one, though. A whole salvo followed, and the camera continued to focus on him in close-up.

Suddenly, however, it panned across the study to the door.

And in strode Martha.

Armed with a tray bearing a tumbler of water and a tube of tablets, she made straight for the desk.

"What do *you* want?" the mayor demanded, dabbing his nose with a handkerchief. "You're intruding."

"Maybe," said Martha, "but you must take your medication." She deposited the tray on the desk. "You're ill, or have you forgotten? Not a wink of sleep all last night. I'd take your medication if I were you."

She eyed the mayor sharply. He stopped dabbing his nose and glowered at her.

"You want to feel better, don't you?"

Slowly at first, then with greater conviction, the mayor nodded.

He popped a tablet into his mouth and washed it down with water. Now it was Martha's turn to nod. She picked up the tray and marched out.

"Well?" said Linda, when she'd gone. "What about those hamster traps?"

The mayor laid his hands one upon the other. "To be honest, we don't know," he said, gazing at the camera as sincerely as he knew how. "I presume, however, that they were set by animal conservationists. With a view to catching any hamsters that happen to be living there."

"Oh?" The camera pulled back to reveal Linda as well as the mayor. "Does that mean you think it's possible that there *are* some field hamsters living on the construction site?"

"I can't judge, being a layman. I have to be guided by what the experts say. But" – the mayor folded his hands on his paunch – "even experts can make mistakes, can't they?" He smiled. "These animal conservationists evidently believe in the hamsters' existence. In other words, doubts have arisen."

"You could always ignore those doubts."

"Miss Carson, I hope you aren't insinuating that I'd wipe out a colony of hamsters, just like that?"

Linda didn't bat an eye. "Of course not, Your Honour. Far be it from me to suggest that you'd deliberately break the law."

"Good." The mayor sat up straight. "That being so, I've come to the following decision: a new scientific inquiry will be held. At the same time, attention will be devoted to the question of whether, and how, any hamsters present on the site can be resettled elsewhere."

The mayor sat back with a friendly smile. "Until that question is resolved, construction work will naturally be suspended."

MY FEET SCARCELY TOUCHED THE GROUND in the two weeks that followed. I mean, it's nice to feel you're needed, but you can also have too much of a good thing. "Operation Resettlement" claimed all my time. I organized, made arrangements, acted as interpreter and heaven knows what else.

Thanks to Linda, the operation began only three days after the TV programme. She dug up a professor of zoology who was reputed to be a hamster expert (as much of a hamster expert as any human can be), and he promptly certified (a) that there were hamsters living in the field, (b) that they could be resettled, and (c) that this must be done at once, or they wouldn't have time to stock up with food for the winter.

Linda then introduced the professor to Jenny. Her detailed knowledge of field-hamster behaviour impressed him so much that he had no hesitation in advising the mayor to put her in charge of the resettlement programme. Which His Honour duly did.

The mayor was relieved that things were moving

Resettlement

so fast because the firm intending to build the automobile plant had been threatening to sue City Hall for compensation if the project was delayed. He also enjoyed being publicly acclaimed as:

"Saviour of the Hamsters"

(by a mass-circulation newspaper, not by Linda) and swiftly declared the resettlement programme a municipal conservation project. This meant that the farmer whose wheat field the hamsters moved to would be compensated for any reduction in its yield.

As for where in the field the hamsters should be permitted to dig their new burrows and how the land should be divided up between them, it goes without saying that these questions provided my cousins with a welcome opportunity to squabble. Jenny (I interpreted for her) learned a great deal about hamster psychology that didn't appear in her zoology book.

I should add that, although they held no official appointment, Frank and Jake also took part in the operation – in fact, I venture to say that we'd never have managed without them. The only little problem was that Jake started cussing whenever Eddy showed up. Eddy and Jenny had fallen for each other, and Princess Sonia declared that their relationship had her blessing. Jenny had a very interesting personal aroma, she said, and would undoubtedly make her master a good mate.

And Fronso? Opinions are divided. Some say he was buried alive, others swear they saw him later and are convinced he escaped. Whatever the truth, a field hamster deprived of the company of other field hamsters is done for in any case.

Then came the day when Operation Resettlement was complete. All the field hamsters had moved into their freshly dug burrows and stowed away the stores they'd brought with them, and all knew where their neighbours lived (so that they could steer clear of them).

It only remained to bid the old field goodbye.

HOW?

By throwing a big farewell party.

CHAPTER FIFTEEN

IN RETROSPECT, Sir William described the party as riotous. My own description of it is more restrained. I won't quote Enrico and Caruso's verdict on it. Being proud of their performance that night, they're naturally biased.

At the field hamsters' request, the party was a purely animal affair and took place in the big cavern where the Jar of Hope still lay empty on its side near the pedestal. It now served only as a hideaway for couples in search of privacy (yes, there was even some smooching on this special occasion).

To enable Sir William to attend, the field hamsters had widened one of their tunnels. It was a tight squeeze, but he made it. "I suppose I ought to think myself lucky, Freddy," he said when he finally reached the cavern. "I'm probably the only tomcat in the world to have visited a hamsters' cathedral."

207

When everyone had assembled, Dolores and Denzil mounted the pedestal. "Hamsters of the field!" cried Dolores, and silence fell. "We want this party to be really enjoyable – and, above all, harmonious."

"Yes," said Denzil, "no insults tonight – none of this 'You stink' and lies of that kind."

"What do you mean, 'lies'? Saying you stink is the plain truth.

"How dare

you! Just you wait, you. . ." Denzil broke off. The two of them looked at each other, then burst out laughing.

"OK," Denzil announced. "Just so you all know what to expect, our festivities will be divided into three parts."

"Yes," said Dolores, "and the first part is an opera."

A long, drawn-out **"Аа ан!"** ran around the cavern. (How did the field hamsters know what

an opera was? Enrico and Caruso had naturally taken the precaution of enlightening them. They didn't want to risk another flop.)

"The second part," said Denzil, "will be a surprise."

"And the third part," said Dolores, "can be summed up as follows: let your hair down!"

"Now for the opera," said Denzil.

"Its title" – Dolores paused for effect – "is *Doña Elvira, or the Power of Destiny.*"

She and Denzil bowed and vacated the pedestal.

Their place was taken by Elvira. A mountainous figure, she sat there flapping a paper fan (which Linda had folded for her) and rolling her eyes with an air of boredom. She was clearly playing a Spanish señora waiting for something to enliven her uneventful existence.

And something did: Don Enrico appeared. Planting

210

himself in front of Doña Elvira, he broke into song (it was an opera, after all):

"Elvira, when I saw you dance
I fell into a kind of trance."

There he stood, little Don Enrico, his red-and-white fur concealing a rather scrawny body — hardly the heart's desire of a Spanish señora waiting for something to dispel her boredom. Sure enough, Doña Elvira had reservations about him. But instead of telling him what they were — or rather, expressing them in song — she resorted to a zoological argument. As she pointed out more than once, she was a hamster and he a guinea pig:

"No, no, alas, it cannot be!
No guinea pig will do for me!"

Scrawny little Don Enrico cut to the quick. Despairingly, he sang:

"Take pity, lady, on my plight
and let our souls in love unite."

But Doña Elvira could not be persuaded. Then came
a duet sung by the two of them in turn:

"To my regret, the fates ordain
that you and i just friends remain!"
"Just friends? I want you for my wife.
That is my one desire in life."
"Your heart, Enrico, may be big,
but you are just a guinea pig."

At this, spontaneous applause erupted. The hamsters
clapped their paws together, as did Sir William. (So did I,
although I found the words rather banal.)

Sadly, Don Enrico turned away. He had no answer to
the zoological argument: destiny had doomed him to be
a guinea pig, and that was that.

Doña Elvira went back to fanning herself and rolling

her eyes. At this point, Don Caruso made his entrance. He too, declared in song that the sight of Doña Elvira dancing had driven him mad with love for her.

There he stood, a stout but imposing figure, and Doña Elvira gazed at him with approval. She played coy nonetheless:

"oh, surely not! it can't be true
that i've enslaved the likes of you!"

But Don Caruso managed to reassure her:

"Together we'll the fates defy,
the perfect couple, you and I."

After which they joined in another duet:

"You love me? can it really be?"
"May lightning strike me if I lie!"
"Are we to marry, you and i?"

213

"Yes, yes, for all eternity!"

"I take you, then, with all my heart."

"And we will never, never part."

There was more applause at this, from me as well (although Caruso had hammed it up a bit too much for my taste).

But what of Don Enrico? Doña Elvira's acceptance of Don Caruso proved that her zoological argument had been just an excuse! Incandescent with rage, Don Enrico challenged his rival to a duel with swords (wheat straws). The outcome was sadly predictable: bravely though he fought, little Don Enrico stood no chance. He was soon stretched out on the ground, breathing his last. Don Caruso turned to his beloved with an air of triumph.

But Don Enrico summoned up his last reserves of strength and struggled to his feet. Doña Elvira had wounded him so deeply that fair play meant nothing to him any more. He skewered Don Caruso in the back and sank to the ground once more.

There the two rivals lay.

Doña Elvira's grief was almost uncontrollable. She gave expression to it in an aria that has since become famous:

"oh, cruel fate!
i'm on my own
without a mate
and all alone.
Bereft of choice,
i end my life
and still my voice
with this sharp knife."

Whereupon – but not before announcing her

intention several times over — she stabbed herself in the bosom.

The ensuing applause was thunderous, as the reader may imagine. Sir William too, was carried away, and so was I (wholeheartedly this time).

Then came the final trio. They sang it lying down, merely raising their heads:

"The three of us are now, alas,
as dead as doornails. Nonetheless,
why should we lament our lot?
Hamster or guinea pig, so what?
Furry or bristly, big or small,
death makes monkeys of us all."

Having reprised this several times, they slowly lowered their heads and expired for good.

The field hamsters went wild, and when Elvira and Enrico and Caruso rose and bowed, their jubilation knew no bounds. Sir William joined in the applause, but with dignity and restraint. And I? I naturally applauded too — after all, one doesn't like to be a party pooper. Just between ourselves, though, I didn't care for the words of the trio. I have no time for the belief that everything is governed by fate. No hamster worthy of the name resigns himself to his fate; he takes it into his own paws.

It was a considerable time before peace returned. Then Dolores and Denzil mounted the pedestal once more.

"And now," said Dolores, "comes the surprise."

"We wanted to thank our human and animal rescuers by presenting them with a gift," said Denzil.

"But there are too many of them," said Dolores. "So we settled on someone who could accept the gift on behalf of the rest."

"And that someone," said Denzil, "is . . . Freddy!"

To me, at least, this came as a genuine surprise. I was

invited on to the pedestal, and Dolores went on, "We wondered what to give Freddy. A MEDAL?"

"But then," said Denzil, "we asked ourselves what would please him most."

Two hamsters approached bearing half a walnut shell covered with wisps of hay. But . . . whatever was in the nutshell was moving! And the aroma it gave off! Abruptly, the hamsters brushed the hay aside.

A loud "Ooooh!" went up from the spectators.

Wriggling around in front of me was a plump, delicious, ENORMOUS MAGGOT.

The field hamsters stared up at me expectantly. I wanted to thank them, but words failed me. I cleared my throat. "Well, I honestly don't know what to say — I mean, how to thank you all, and——"

"So don't bother," boomed Elvira. "Just do what a hamster normally does to a maggot!"

Which I proceeded to do on the pedestal itself, with everyone watching.

Then came the third part of the festivities.

Today, when the field hamsters talk about their "Grand Farewell Gala", this is really the part they mean. They danced and sang, squabbled and made up, until the cavern rang with the din. Above all, they gorged themselves. It turned out that they'd left some hoarded food behind in their old burrows – not just some but plenty, and all, it transpired as the night wore on, of the finest quality. And we polished off every last morsel.

I can only tell you this: any hamster who splurges the contents of his larder is *really* celebrating!

CHAPTER SIXTEEN

THE NEXT DAY, I was working out on my hamster carousel, a circular disc of wood mounted at a slight angle so it turns when I run on it. The carousel is wonderful for jogging, and it's still my favourite piece of sports equipment.

So there I was, jogging in my cage on Mr John's bookshelf, when I was hailed from below.

"Freddy?"

Enrico and Caruso. What did *they* want? They'd probably been hatching some new guinea-piggish plot. Well, this time they'd be disappointed – I wasn't going to play their game. Still, I could hardly pretend I hadn't heard them. I'm a civilized domestic animal, after all. Reluctantly, I got off the carousel and looked down, all my senses on the alert. "What do you want?" I asked curtly.

"We wanted to tell you something, but not from

down here, it's so demeaning.
Could you join us for a few moments?
We know it's asking a lot, but this is
important."

Very well. Being a civilized domestic animal carried certain responsibilities. Peevishly, I climbed down my rope ladder to the floor. Heaven help them if what they had to tell me was unimportant.

"Well?" I said. My mental command centre had issued a Red Alert.

"Freddy," said Enrico, "you may have noticed how seriously we took that operatic performance of ours at the field hamsters' party."

I nodded. That was undeniable.

"The opera being our first major work," said Caruso, "it made us realize that, from now on, we shall have to be mindful of our artistic reputation."

I nodded again. I really couldn't dispute that.

"And that," Enrico announced, "is why we've been rethinking our relationship with you."

"Oh?" I said.

"Yes," said Caruso. "We mean the tasteless practical jokes we've taken the liberty of playing on you."

"Oh?" Sirens started blaring in my head, and an illuminated sign flashed the word **ALERT!** in big red letters.

"We've been counting up," Enrico confessed, "and we find we bugged you six times in the course of that field hamster episode."

"*Six* times!" I exclaimed.

I was genuinely surprised. I'd have put it at far fewer, but then, I'm the forgiving type.

"First of all," Caruso recalled, "I imitated that cry for help. A thoroughly mean trick."

"You could call it that," I said. When they were right, they were right.

"Then there was 'When Freddy puts his paw down,

it means he's laid the law down'," said Enrico, counting. "Kindergarten humour, I'd call that."

Nothing to disagree with there.

."Next: 'Life's an adventure, friends.'" Caruso hesitated. "Not bad, until we got to the bit about hamsters being small and timid. That was downright offensive."

Equally correct, but I was beginning to wonder why they were reciting all this stuff.

"Then came two more lines," said Enrico, still counting. "'Our hamster expert likes to brag' and 'Our celebrated author's paw'. Extremely tasteless, especially when one remembers your predicament on the second occasion."

Quite right. The only thing was, what the heck were they getting at?

"Last of all," Caruso said, "our 'Third Man' skit. Not only tasteless but malicious."

"I quite agree," I said, but I was growing impatient.

What were they playing at? If the whole thing was leading up to some guinea-piggishness on their part, heaven help them! I would forget I was courteous and civilized – Sir William happened to be asleep, fortunately – and bite them with a ferocity worthy of my ancestors. "Look, you guys," I said, controlling myself with difficulty, "why are you telling me all this?"

"Didn't we say?" Enrico asked in surprise. "We're trying to draw a line under our disreputable past."

"Which means," Caruso amplified, "that we won't bug you any more in the future."

"I'll believe that when it doesn't happen," I retorted angrily. "It's easy to talk."

"We didn't think you'd believe us," said Enrico. "We simply wanted to tell you."

"And that's all?" I snapped.

"Yes," Caruso said quietly.

"You got me down here just for *that*?!" I demanded with mounting anger. "Just to tell me something I wouldn't believe?" I turned away. "I refuse to be taken for a fool." Fuming, I started back up my rope ladder. Guinea pigs! I fall for yet another of their tricks, and they give me a load of hot air about playing no more tricks in the future. Incredible! To think I'd interrupted my workout for *that*!

I was so incensed by the time I reached my cage, I gave a furious snarl. Those confounded guinea pigs never failed to . . . . I stopped short.

A derisive chorus came drifting up from below:

"But oh, a hamster blind with rage
we find the funniest sight of all. . ."

This was followed by the inevitable squeals of laughter.

For fear of perpetrating a frightful massacre down there, I had to cling to one of the cage bars with my teeth. I almost exploded with the fury that was blazing and bubbling away inside me. If I'd let go of the cage bar, I'd probably have shot upwards like a rocket, heading to

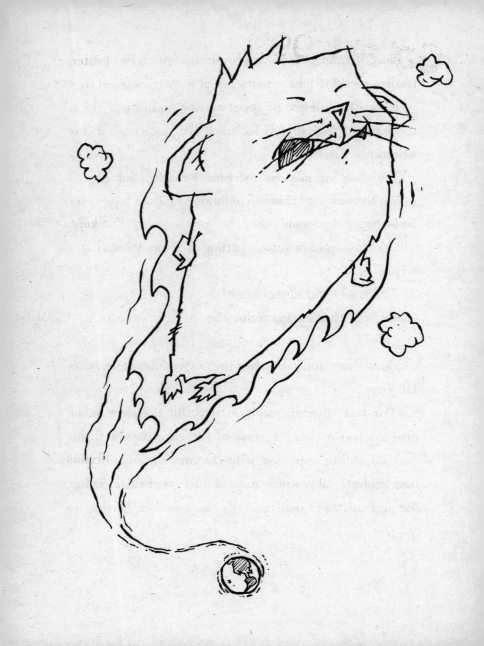

Galaxy 999, and throttled its sinister

inhabitant with my bare paws.

Its sinister inhabitant? Just a minute.

I let go of the cage bar and sat down.

But of course!

The sinister being really existed.

Not somewhere in space, though.

He was here in my cage. The sinister being who kept telling those guinea pigs how best to bug me was . . . myself.

Sophie was planning to pay me a visit that afternoon.

I'd got everything ready hours beforehand. I'd also conducted several rehearsals and discussed matters with Mr John. Now I was restlessly scurrying to and fro.

"My dear Freddy," said Sir William. "Driving us all mad won't make her show up any sooner."

The waiting was over at last, however: Sophie came hurrying into the study accompanied by her titillating scent of sunflower seeds.

"Hello, Freddy!" she called.

She'd spotted me at once, even though I wasn't in my cage. I was sitting on the desk beside the keyboard. The computer wasn't on, of course.

As usual when Sophie called "Hello, Freddy!" I sat up and begged. I always do that — it's part of our ritual. After that, our ritual prescribes that I raise my right paw as high as I can. Then I wave.

But this time I didn't wave.

I sat up on my haunches, but my paw stayed down.

Sophie, who had already opened her mouth to exclaim "He's waving!" stopped short. She shook her head uncertainly.

"Freddy?" she said, coming closer. "What's wrong? Why no welcome?"

And then — I was right beside it — I pressed the computer's start button.

The machine came on with a loud *Bong!* and the screen lit up. It took some time (I avoided looking at Sophie meanwhile) for the program to load itself.

Then I started. As fast as I could — I wanted her just to watch, not think too much — I wrote the following on the screen:

> This hamster has the happy knack,
> when greeting folk, of waving back.
> But why, though, purely for a change,
> should Freddy not extend his range?
> It's true he cannot beautify
> his greeting with a dulcet cry;
> he cannot bark like dog or hound,
> nor yet produce a whistling sound
> like mynah birds, nor can he purr
> like pussycats that clean their fur,

nor imitate a guinea pig
(for that he doesn't give a fig),
nor splash like goldfish in a bowl,
nor hoot in welcome like an owl,
nor yet, as turtledoves will do,
can Freddy very softly coo.
He's able to do none of these,
but he can read and write with ease.
You must have noticed that already,
so please congratulate your—

"Freddy!" exclaimed Sophie.

I straightened up, raised one paw, and waved.

"You're waving!" she cried. "You're saying hello after all!" She broke off and smiled at me.

Puzzled, I lowered my

paw. Didn't she realize what she'd just witnessed? A golden hamster had welcomed her with a poem of his own composition! A poem he'd typed on a computer keyboard with his very own paws! I mean, a historic occurrence of such magnitude should have knocked her sideways.

"You can wave and turn somersaults," said Sophie, looking at me gravely, "and now you can read and write as well." She gave a contented nod. "I knew it right away: You're the bestest, smartest golden hamster in the world."

When I'd asked Mr John what he thought of letting Sophie in on my secret after all, he just looked at me thoughtfully for a while. At length he said, "It means a lot to you, doesn't it?"

I nodded.

"Well, kid," he said, "the fact remains, the fewer the people who know about it, the better."

But, Mr John, I typed, *so many people already know — the Muskrats, for example, and Eddy must also have heard what I can do. I don't see why Sophie should be left out.*

"Hmm," said Mr John. He plucked at one of his bushy eyebrows in silence. After a while, he said suddenly, "All right, so be it. But in that case we must reverse our tactics."

I LOOKED PUZZLED.

"Having as few people in the know as possible," he said, "has been your best protection up to now. In the future, it must be as many people as possible — everyone, preferably. Then any no-good person who tries to harm you will have the general public to contend with."

You mean, the general public will get to hear of me?

I typed. *You mean, a hamster named Freddy can now become a celebrated author?*

Mr John laughed. "I don't see why not." Then he turned serious again. "That's settled, then," he said. "There's only one thing."

Which is? I typed.

"When you told me about those cries for help from the field hamsters, I asked you a question."

True. He'd asked me why I wasn't swamped with similar cries for help in Interanimal – with appeals for help from thousands of creatures in distress. Why didn't I hear them *all*? Why didn't other animals hear them?

I still don't have an answer to that, I typed.

"Could it be," he said, "that you've grown deaf, you animals, simply to protect yourselves from such a barrage of cries?"

Maybe, I typed. *But why did we hear those field hamsters?*

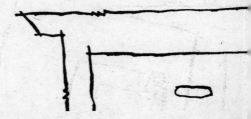

"Perhaps your ears are opening again. Unless they do it'll be too late – too late for you animals to save yourselves." He looked at me. "But even if your hearing *does* improve, it won't do you much good."

HE WAS RIGHT.

It's up to humans.

Humans too, must learn to hear those cries.